DARK COUNTY
ten tales of rural terror
BY KIT TINSLEY

To
Katrina
All the best
Kit Tinsley

COPYRIGHT 2013 Kit Tinsley
Cover Photography: Brad Bourne @ something wicked productions
Edited by Jacqueline DeBella
This book is a work of fiction. Any similarity to any persons living or dead is purely coincidental.
The author holds all rights to this work.

ALSO BY THE AUTHOR

BENEATH

This book is dedicated to
Siobhan and Freddy
My reasons for living

CONTENTS

Introduction - 9

A Drive in the Country 11-

Hoodies - 31

House by the Marsh - 51

Fear and Loathing in Skeg Vegas - 87

Tracks - 113

The Crows - 127

Fear Thy Neighbour - 147

Coffin Hall - 155

What Grows in the Far Field - 165

A Campfire Tale - 185

Afterword - 195

About the Author - 203

INTRODUCTION

I was born in the county of Shropshire, a place I still have a great affection for and honestly believe to be the most beautiful place in England, but I do not consider it my home. When I was seven years old, my father got a job that entailed us moving across the country to Lincolnshire. I went from one rural county to another, though they couldn't be more different. Shropshire has massive hills that are, in fact, the tail end of some of the northern Welsh mountain ranges, and a lot of livestock. Lincolnshire on the other hand is, bar a few places, flat as a pancake, and is mainly used for the growing of crops.

It is in Lincolnshire that I have grown up, stayed for all of these years, and more than likely will stay forever. I am comfortable here, I am happy to raise my son here. It is a pleasant county and truly breathtaking at times. The first thing my family noticed on moving here was how big the skies were. Back in Shropshire, the gargantuan hills eat into the sky like hungry green beasts. In Lincolnshire, there is very little to break up the sky from one horizon to the other. Certain places, like the marshes near Boston, are so vast and flat that you can actually see the curvature of the Earth with the naked eye.

Why are you telling us this, Kit? What has this all got to do with horror stories? Well, I shall tell you. Despite its beauty, there is also an eerie bleakness to the landscape of Lincolnshire. In certain places, you feel utterly isolated and due to the vast skies and open, flat spaces, you also feel small and insignificant.

There is a darkness within the county, a sense of the world passing it by. There are a large number of lovely people in the county, but there are also a lot of small-minded and prejudiced people. It is these contrasts in light and dark, in good and bad, that fascinate me. I can be driving past a farm and my mind wanders and automatically thinks of the worst-case scenario.

That is what inspired this collection of stories, and my previous novel *Beneath*. You see, as much as I love this county and consider it my home, it also frightens me.

The stories you are about to read are varied in their styles and subject matter. They are all horror, but some are psychological, some are visceral. Some are about supernatural evil, others about human evil. What links them all is this county. Each one of them is inspired by a specific place, or event, or image that I have encountered here, and the dark places my mind has taken me.

At the end of the book, you will find an afterword where I will tell you a little more about the places and events that inspired each story. For now, though, sit back and relax, dim the lights and let me take you with me through the craven heart of this dark county. Let's start by taking a pleasant drive in the country.....

A DRIVE IN THE COUNTRY

It was supposed to have been a pleasant, relaxing, Sunday afternoon drive in the country. That's what Mark had promised her, but Kelly now felt more stressed than she had before. Mark had decided to take them well off the beaten track, into the wilds of the marshlands.

'It'll be fun,' he had said as he'd pulled off the A16 onto the first of many narrow, winding lanes. 'Where's your sense of adventure?'

They had eventually come to a dead end in the road. A little, cracked concrete car park lay on the left hand side. Mark had pulled the car over and stopped the engine.

'What are you doing?' she'd asked.

'Come on, let's go for a walk,' he had said, undoing his seatbelt.

'Where?' She replied with a question. She looked around and saw nothing but miles of flat, bleak farmland.

Mark pointed to the grassy bank at the end of the road.

'Over there are the marshes themselves. Let's go and have a look.'

Kelly sighed and undid her seat belt, then reluctantly got out of the car. Despite the warmth of the day, there was a reasonably strong wind blowing and with nothing to dampen its force for miles around, it had a chill to it.

'Christ, it's cold,' Kelly said, hugging herself.

Mark stood straight with his hands resting on his hips, his back arched as he took in a long, deep breath.

'I think they call it bracing,' he said as he exhaled. 'The smell of the country.'

Yes, Kelly had noticed that, too. She had often heard people talk about the wonderful country air, all she could smell was a combination of seawater and shit. She reached into the back seat of the car and picked up her jacket. Slipping it on she felt a little warmer, but it was only a lightweight leather thing designed more for fashion than for protection from the elements. It would not really do that much to keep her warm, but it made her feel a little better.

'Come on, then,' Mark said, taking her hand in his and leading her towards the bank.

As they stepped off the hard concrete of the road, and onto the grassy bank, Kelly felt the ground beneath giving a little too much. She looked down and saw that the thick, black, squelching mud was halfway up her shoes. Thank God she had not worn the sandals she had planned to wear.

At the top of the bank they could see the expanses of marsh spreading out before them. It was a mix of long grass, mud and seawater filling up gaping channels. When the tide was in much of what they saw would be underwater. Kelly wondered how often people got stranded out here, marooned on one of those little islands until the tide retreated, or worse, they drowned in the salty brine. The thought made her shiver.

'See, isn't that impressive?' Mark asked. Kelly could tell that he was desperate for her approval, to see that she was having a good time. She wanted to scream at him that it wasn't impressive, that all she could see was miles and miles of absolutely fuck all, but she didn't. She knew that Mark was trying really hard, he wanted to make things right between them, wanted things to be the way they were before, but he couldn't. No one could. If either of them had caused their problems then maybe it would be different. If Mark had cheated on her, for example, perhaps she could have forgiven him and they could move on, but how do you move on when you miscarry, it was no one's fault. She could not blame Mark, so she could not forgive him.

'Yes, it's impressive,' she said half smiling, trying to reward the effort he was making as much as she could.

'Do you want to walk out there?' he asked motioning towards the expanse.

'No, it might be dangerous,' she said. 'Let's just walk along the bank a little way.'

Mark looked disappointed at first, then his eyes softened, he could see that she was trying, too. He'd always been able to read her so well. He knew that she didn't want to be walking out here at all, but the fact that she agreed to walk along the bank showed that she cared enough to compromise.

They headed east along the bank holding hands in silence. The place was so isolated, Kelly could see that other people came up here, she could tell from the sheer amount of dog crap she had to avoid, but right now they were the only people in sight for miles.

As they walked, the car became a dot in the distance, sat there all alone in the car park. Kelly began to feel better; perhaps Mark had been right all along, the walk seemed to be clearing her head. For weeks now, she had felt so alone, even in crowded rooms. Now out here where she was physically isolated form everyone but Mark, a strange peace began to come over her. She grasped his hand a little tighter and rested her head on his arm as they walked.

Suddenly Mark stopped dead in his tracks.

'What the hell is that?' he said.

At first she could not tell what he was looking at, there was so much nothing that it detracted from what was there. Then she saw it—a full, black refuse sack, sitting in the undergrowth at the bottom of the bank, with what appeared to be blonde hair poking out where it was tied.

'Oh my God, do you think it's...' She couldn't finish the sentence, she could not say the words a body, ridiculous to even think that, it was just some fibre glass insulation or something. Someone had been doing some DIY and rather than take it to the tip they had dumped it out here, inconsiderate yes, but nothing more sinister. Then she noticed the red splatter all over it. Paint. She tried to tell herself that it was just paint, but she knew well enough what blood looked like, she had seen plenty in her career as a nurse, and there had been so much when she miscarried.

'I'd better take a look,' Mark said, letting go of her hand.

'Perhaps we should call the police?' she said.

'Not if it's just some bag of rubbish, we'd be wasting their time. You wait here. I'll go and check it out.'

With that, he was heading down the bank. Kelly stood on the top, suddenly feeling very vulnerable. She could see that there was no one else around, yet she couldn't help feeling as though she were being watched.

She hugged herself again; the wind felt colder all of a sudden.

Mark reached the bottom of the bank and stood over the bag, his face contorted in a grimace. She knew the look well. It was the one he made whenever he smelled something bad. He looked around on the ground, obviously he didn't want to use his hands to open the bag. Eventually he found a piece of wood; he used it to carefully tear open the bag.

He recoiled in horror as the young woman's head rolled out of the bag and fell to his feet. Kelly screamed, a sound that seemed to echo forever in that wide-open nothingness. Mark left the piece of wood on the ground and ran up the bank to her. He wrapped his arms around her and turned her away from the sight of the head.

'It's all right,' he cooed gently, though she could feel his heart thumping in his chest.

'All right?' she sobbed. 'It's a human fucking head!'

'Not just a head,' he said. 'There were all sorts of bits of cut up body in the bag.'

Kelly pulled away from him and doubled over. She heaved once and the vomit poured from her mouth. Mark rubbed her back with one hand whilst holding her hair back with the other. It was not the site of the viscera that made her sick; after all, she had seen plenty of that in her life. It was the shock of seeing something so horrific so unexpectedly. It was also the knowledge that someone had done something so brutal and horrendous.

'Do you have your phone?' he said. 'I left mine on charge at home.'

Without standing up, Kelly rummaged in her jacket pocket. She found the phone and passed it to her husband before another wave of sick erupted from her mouth.

'No signal,' he said.

'What do we do?'

'We get back to the car, keep trying the phone. When we have a signal we'll stop and call the police.'

'What if we don't get a signal? We're out in the arse end of nowhere!' she said.

'Then we drive till we find a police station. We're not far from a town. Maybe six miles that way,' he pointed past where the car was parked.

They hurried back to where the car was parked, on that little patch of concrete. All the way there, Kelly kept the phone in her hand, constantly checking for the signal symbol to appear. Even if there were no bars, if that little symbol appeared she would be able to call the emergency services. It did not appear.

They jumped into the car. Mark pulled away before she had even fastened her seat belt. He drove far too fast. It was unlike him; he was usually such a cautious driver. She would often tease him about driving like an old woman, but now it was like he was rally driving.

Still her phone was useless, the signal symbol refusing to make an appearance. Mark swung the car around a hairpin bend; she heard the tyres screeching as they tried desperately to keep contact with the road and felt gravity throw her against her window, bumping her head.

'Slow down!'

Mark looked at her.

'I just want to get as far away from there as I can,' he said, his gaze never leaving her. Out of the corner of her eye, she saw a dark shape appear on the road.

'Look out!' she yelled, but it was too late.

The impact was deafening, the crunch of metal and the smash of glass. The windscreen shattered as the object bounced off the bonnet then rolled onto the roof. The brakes screamed as Mark brought the car to a sudden halt.

'Was that a person?' she asked, not wanting to look back.

'I don't know,' Mark said. 'Wait here while I check.'

He undid his seatbelt and opened the car door.

'I'm coming with you,' she said. 'I am a nurse, after all.'

Together they walked slowly back to the spot where the thing that they had hit lay slumped on the road. As they got closer Kelly could see, to her horror, that it was wearing clothes, and hence a human being. There was a small amount of blood sprayed around the body. It was face down on the ground, she could not tell if it was a man or woman, the hair was fairly long, but greasy and matted.

'Are they alive?' Mark asked. 'Please, God, let them be alive.'

Kelly took hold of the person's wrist and could feel a fairly strong pulse. She was relieved enough to let out a loud sigh.

'There's a pulse,' she said.

'Thank Christ.'

The wrist that she was holding was suddenly tugged out of her grasp. The person was moving; they rolled over and looked around. Kelly could see that it was a young man, probably no more than twenty, though determining his exact age was impossible. His face was a road map of scar tissue. One ear was almost completely missing, just a few bits of tattered flesh protruding. Also one cheekbone seemed much larger than the other, as thought it had been shattered at some point and then left to heal wrong. The nose was flat and crooked; it had obviously been broken numerous times in the past and judging from the blood running freely, was broken again. Several teeth were missing. There were a few fresh cuts, yet most of the wounds seemed old and badly healed.

'Sorry,' the young man said. 'I weren't looking where I were going.'

His accent was thick Lincolnshire, and he sounded a little slow.

'It's all right,' Kelly said. 'Just try not to move, we'll call you an ambulance.'

She threw her phone to Mark.

'What's your name?' Kelly asked.

'Peter,' The young man replied. 'But most people just call me Smash.'

'Okay, Smash,' It felt wrong calling him that, considering the state his body was in from wounds old and new, she guessed this was the reason for the nickname.

'Still no signal,' Mark said.

'How old are you, Smash?' Kelly asked to check to see if he was in any state of confusion.

'Sixteen, Miss,' the boy replied.

'Do you think you can walk?' Kelly asked.

The boy nodded and started to rise to his feet. Kelly put her arm around him for support. When he was upright, she could see that his legs could take his weight, suggesting that neither they nor his hips were broken. They started slowly moving to the car. The boy was limping, but it didn't seem to be causing him any pain. This made her think that the limp had been there already, a result of the previous accident that had left him so mangled.

'Get him in the back seat,' Mark said, opening the door. 'We'll take him to the hospital. We can call the police from there about the body in the bag.'

The boy stood up straight, stopping in dead.

'No, I'm not going to the hospital,' he said emphatically.

'You've just been hit by a car at pretty high speed,' Kelly said.

'Just a few bumps and bruises,' the boy said, shrugging it off.

'You could have internal bleeding. A doctor really should take a look at you,' Kelly persisted.

'No fucking hospital!' the boy shouted furiously. Kelly was taken aback by the sudden rage. Mark took a step closer, to intervene if need be. The boy, however, instantly calmed down.

'I'm really sorry,' he said. 'I just don't like hospitals. I'm fine, really, if you could just give me a lift home.'

'We really need to speak to the police,' Mark said.

'I only live up the road,' the boy said. 'You can use our phone.'

Mark looked annoyed; he was obviously eager to get away from there, but Kelly nodded. It would be the quickest way to get hold of the police. Mark sighed.

'Okay,' he said. 'Get in.'

Kelly helped the boy lower himself onto the back seat, she was about to get in there with him so that she could keep an eye on him for signs of injury, but Mark gently pulled on her arm and nodded towards the front passenger seat. Typical Mark, he was overcautious, he never trusted anyone, but considering what they had been through already today she nodded acceptance and got into the front of the car.

The boy, Smash, directed them up the road about half a mile and then told them to take the next right. The road, if you could call it that, was little more than a dirt track that ran alongside a field of golden wheat. It went on for about a mile. The car bumped down the road; it would be doing the suspension no good. She considered telling Mark to slow down, but could see from the look on his face his was determined to get there as quick as possible.

The house came into view on the right. It was a large Victorian-built farmhouse. With the right love and attention, it could have been a beautiful home. Instead, it was a weather- and time-battered heap. Brickwork was falling away on the side, the chimney was protruding at such an angle that it seemed to be defying the laws of physics by staying up on the broken roof. Several windows were broken and just left boarded up, and the whole thing was covered by brown, skeletal and long-dead ivy. Outside the house were a couple of beaten up old Land Rovers, a rusting white Mercedes van and a tractor that looked as though it had been bought when most people were still using horses and carts. A pair of shirtless and grubby looking children ran around the overgrown garden. Kelly guessed they were Smash's younger siblings; they had the same dark, greasy hair that seemed to have been just left to grow with no particular style.

Mark pulled up next to one of the Land Rovers. The somewhat feral-looking children stared over at them, but made no attempt to approach. Mark turned off the engine and opened the door.

'Wait in the car,' he said to Kelly as he helped Smash out of the back seat.

'No chance,' she said, getting out herself.

Smash led them to the front door. As he opened it, Kelly was hit by the smell from inside, a combination of body odour, cooking meat and something else she couldn't quite place.

'Come in,' Smash said to them as he limped through the door. 'Mum, I got company.'

The woman who stepped out into the hallway was enormous. She was at least twenty-five stone. She wore a dirty, yellow, floral print dress that looked more like a bed sheet than actual clothing. Her hair was dark and wildly curly. Her piggy features were virtually being swallowed up by the fat of her cheeks. Her jowls hung low, giving her the appearance of having no neck, just a fat head melding into a fat body. Her arms were covered in faded, blue and obviously home done tattoos. She gave off an aroma that was like rotting fish in gone off cheese, undoubtedly caused by the build up of mouldy yeast that inhabited her gargantuan rolls of fat.

'What ya done to ya sen now?' she said in accent even thicker than her son's. It had always confused Kelly the way that Lincolnshire people used the word 'sen' instead of self.

'I had an accident,' Smash said gingerly.

'Yes, I'm so sorry but we hit your son with our car,' Kelly said. 'I think he might need a doctor, but he refused to go to the hospital.'

The woman walked over and grabbed Smash's face, turning it from side to side.

'No harm done,' she said. 'Bet you weren't looking where you were going, were you?'

'No, Mum,' Smash said.

'I'm a nurse and I would advise you to take him to the hospital,' Kelly said.

'He's fine,' the woman snapped, then added more gently, 'he's had a lot worse.'

Kelly could blatantly see that this was true. She wanted to ask how he had got the other wounds he had, but felt that it would be prying, and that this was a woman who would not take kindly to prying.

'Of course,' Kelly said.

'Thank you for bringing him home, duck,' she said. 'Can I offer you a cuppa?'

The idea of drinking anything prepared by this monstrous woman, or in this filthy house, made her stomach do a little flip. If she hadn't already been sick on the marsh, she would have thrown up right there.

'No, thanks,' Mark responded for them both, 'but I do need to use your phone.'

'Yes, we need to call the police,' Kelly added.

'The police?' the woman said, concerned.

'Yes, we found...' Kelly was going to say it, but something made her hold back. 'We found something on the marsh they need to know about.'

The woman looked from her to Mark and then back.

'All right,' she said finally. 'Smash, show him where the phone is.'

'Yes, Mum,' he said, leading Mark off down the hall.

Kelly was about to follow when the woman stepped in her path.

'Why don't you wait in the living room with me?' she said. 'It's not often we have visitors.'

Kelly really didn't want to, but smiled politely and followed the woman into the living room.

It was a cluttered and dusty mess, a large room with several mismatched sofas. An enormous, dark wood dresser took up most of one wall, the kind of thing that people would use to display their finest China, but instead this one was empty. It stood there looming over the room like an ominous shadow. The carpet was threadbare and stained with God only knew what.

Kelly sat down on the sofa opposite the woman. This was one of the rooms with boarded windows, it made the air heavy and the woman's stench even more potent. She was eating from a large plate of meat; to Kelly it looked like it was most likely pork though she was not sure what cut.

She offered the plate to Kelly, who put her hand up to refuse it.

'Vegetarian,' she lied.

'No wonder you're so skinny.' The woman said, laughing as she took a handful of meat. Kelly didn't see herself as that skinny, but she supposed that to this behemoth she looked like one of those size zero models.

There was a clock on the wall behind her and it ticked loudly. The woman did not try to engage her in conversation; instead, she just sat there chewing her meat, slapping her chops as she did. The combination of that and the sound of the clock quickly became maddening. Tick, slap, tock, slap, tick, slap, tock, slap, tick and on and on. Kelly felt more on edge than she could remember ever being before. Something was wrong here, very wrong, the way the woman just stared at her as she chewed. She hoped that Mark would hurry back, that they could leave this house, leave this whole fucking area behind and go home.

'Could I use your bathroom?' Kelly said, wanting to get out of the room and away from the woman's unflinching gaze.

'Bathroom's upstairs, but there's a shitter just across the hall,' the woman said.

Kelly faked a laugh politely and then got out of the room. She stood in the hallway, she strained to listen for the sound of Mark's voice, but she couldn't. A strange feeling came over her like she had experienced out on the marsh, that feeling of being watched. She looked up and saw the two children she had seen outside were silently observing her from the stairs. Now that she saw them more clearly, she could tell that they were twin boys, identical twin boys. She guessed that they were around nine or ten years old. She smiled at them. They just continued to stare at her.

She went into the small toilet under the stairs. The toilet itself was filthy, caked in shit and swarming with flies. The nausea returned, she covered her mouth and closed her eyes, concentrating on not being sick. After a few moments, she felt a little better. It was hard for her, a nurse married to a man who ran his own successful consulting firm, to imagine that there were still people living like this nowadays. It was as if when she stepped through the front door of this house she had gone back in time a hundred years, or been magically transported to a third world country.

She decided that her best course of action was to wait in here until she heard Mark in the hallway, then she could step out and they could leave. It stank in the small cramped toilet, and she was sure that just breathing the air could give her dysentery, but it sure beat sitting opposite the woman as she pushed handfuls of meat into her monstrous mouth or standing in the hallway being studied by those creepy twins.

How long she stayed there she wasn't sure, but it must have been at least ten minutes, and still there was no sign of Mark's return. This was getting ridiculous, what could be taking him so long? Given the nature of what they had found on the marsh surely the police would want to get out there quickly, not keep Mark on the phone for so long.

She opened the door quietly, hoping not to make the woman in the living room aware of her movement. For a moment as she pulled the door slowly opened, she imagined the woman stood outside the door waiting for her, still stuffing her face with the meat. However, the hallway was empty, a great relief. Kelly stepped out of the toilet and turned to look up. The twins had gone.

When they had arrived, Smash had led Mark to the room at the end of the hallway to use the phone. Kelly decided to go down there and see what was taking so long. She walked on tiptoes trying to make as little noise as possible. When she reached the door, she turned the handle slowly, pulling the door open. The room was a kitchen, or at least as near to a kitchen as this hellhole could offer. The floor was covered in faded green vinyl that felt sticky under her feet, like the floor of one of the grim pubs she frequented in her college days. The worktops were littered with pots and crockery that looked as though they had not been washed in decades. A group of mangy looking cats were licking crusted food off the plates. Mark, however, along with Smash was nowhere to be seen.

The phone was attached to the wall on the other side of the room. Kelly walked over to it, hoping that Mark was on the phone in another room, suddenly she longed to hear her husband's voice. The phone was dead, not even a dial tone. There was a door that led out to the rear of the house, and another that led down a set of stairs to a cellar. She could think of no good reason why Mark would be in the cellar, but she was running out of options so she walked to the door and listened carefully. Though she could not hear her husband talking, there was a sound coming from below. A frequent wet bang, like you would hear in a butcher's shop.

Fear told her to run to the back door and exit the house now, nothing good could come from that sound. What would she do when she got outside? Mark had the car keys, would she just run aimlessly through the fields?

Smash appeared at the bottom of the stairs. He was wearing a blood soaked apron, and carrying in one hand a meat cleaver and in the other a black refuse sack dripping with blood.

'Stay calm, Miss,' he said when he saw her at the top of the stairs, looking down at him with an open mouth.

For a moment, she was paralysed. Grief, horror, and self-preservation were all vying for control of her emotions. Smash dropped the sack to the floor and started up the stairs. Kelly saw Mark's head roll from the sack.

'You monster!' she cried out. Her mind cleared, self-preservation had won the battle and she turned to run, only to find the woman behind her brandishing a mallet. The woman was wild as she swung the mallet at her, but Kelly was a lot quicker than this hulking creature. She ducked, avoiding the swing by inches. The woman had put such force into the swing that she was momentarily off balance, it was just the advantage that Kelly needed. She shoulder barged the unstable woman towards the cellar stairs; the woman screamed as she fell down the stairs, knocking her son to the floor as she did.

Kelly looked down and saw that the woman wasn't moving. Smash, on the other hand, was getting to his feet. Needing no more motivation, Kelly bounded for the back door, only to find it was locked. She could hear Smash ascending the stairs quickly. She elbowed the large glass pane on the door and it shattered violently outward, she knew that she had some nasty cuts on her arm from doing this that would need stitching, but now was not the time to worry about that.

She climbed through the broken door, cutting herself again on the broken glass. She fell to the ground but instantly got to her feet. Looking back, she saw that Smash was in the kitchen now, heading for the door. She took off, running as quickly as she could.

She knew that the road was at least a mile back up the dirt track, but it was an isolated country lane. There was no guarantee that she would find help that way, besides which she wanted to run away from the house, not around the side of it. She headed straight, away from the back of the house, hoping that she would come to another road or another house. She looked back to see Smash was climbing through the broken door. He hit the ground running, and he was quick, she pushed herself harder hoping to keep ahead of him. She saw a hedgerow up ahead, this must mark the end of the property. She prayed that there was a road the other side of it.

Looking back, she saw that Smash was gaining on her, despite his limp when walking, he ran like a big cat hunting its pray. The hedgerow was no more than a hundred meters away when she stumbled, her ankle twisting in a rabbit hole. The pain was immense. She kept her balance and managed to stay upright, but the delay cost her dearly.

She turned to see Smash right behind her. He swung the meat cleaver and it connected with her side, just below her rib cage. It must have gone a good three inches into her body. The pain was like a fire in her side. Smash pulled the cleaver back out of her. She clutched the wound and felt the blood pouring over her hand. Smash prepared to take another swing with the cleaver, the one that would end her for sure. Without a second's hesitation Kelly kicked out, her foot connecting full force with Smash's groin. He screamed in pain and the cleaver went flying from his grasp, far off into the distance. The last time she had inflicted this pain on a man he had dropped to his knees instantly, then fallen to the ground writhing in agony. Smash, though, was made of stronger stuff. He grabbed at his groin and bent over, but he did not drop to the floor.

'You bitch!' He screamed. 'I'm going to skin you alive for that.'

He made a grab for her arm, but she avoided him, it was clear she was going to have to keep running. The pain in her side was going numb, she knew all too well that this was a bad sign, her body was going into shock. Not only that but she knew she was losing too much blood too rapidly, if she didn't get help soon she would bleed out, the dizziness she was starting to feel was a symptom of this. She pushed on through it, keeping her eyes on the hedgerow. Smash had begun to chase her again, but the kick to the balls had slowed him down. She would make it to the hedgerow before him.

She heard the sound of an engine in the distance; there was a road on the other side of the hedgerow. She made it to the thick hedge of brambles and pushed her way through. The thorns scratching her were nothing compared to the wound on her side. She barely even felt it. She saw the road ahead of her and ran for it. Unfortunately, she did not see the dyke between her and the road. She fell straight into it, her damaged body hitting the dry bottom with a thud. She tried to clamber up the side of the dyke, but her strength was leaving her, her body was shutting down to protect itself from the injury. She heard a thump behind her. Turning, she saw Smash had jumped into the dyke. He smiled at her.

'Still with us, Miss?' he said cheerfully. 'Good, good. We'll have some fun later, but there's something I have to do first.' With that, he climbed out of the dyke leaving her where she lay.

She heard the sound of the engine very close, then the screech of brakes and the thump of a boy against metal.

She heard voices. She tried to cry out, but she could not. Her lungs had started to fill with blood.

'Oh fuck!' A woman said hysterically. 'Is he dead? Did I kill him?'

'I don't know,' a man said.

After a pause, she heard a familiar voice.

'Sorry,' Smash said. 'I weren't looking where I were going.'

Tears filled Kelly's eyes as the lights began to fade.

HOODIES

The nighttime Streets of Darton were bathed in the sickly, orange glow of the street lamps. Benton roamed the streets with the gang, all of them dressed in their jogging bottoms, baseball caps and hoodies. They wandered around like a pack of sneering jackals, taunting those who crossed their path. They lived for the fear they instilled in the hearts of others. Like so many youths from the wrong estates, it was the only power they would ever feel.

Tonight was the first time that Benton had been included in the gang. Before tonight, he had always been well behaved and hardworking at school, but to what end? To his teachers he was invisible just because of the geography of his home. It seemed like his postcode had determined his destiny. He was to be at best overlooked his entire life, at worst judged as a thug. So why not follow the path that society seemed determined for him to take?

When he was a young child, his best friend had been Steve Murphy, the boy next door. As they had grown older, though, Steve had set off on the road to villainy. He became a bully and a troublemaker. His family had a reputation as thugs and criminals, and it was one that Steve was happy to live up to. Though the same age as Benton, Steve had already left school, not officially, just in the sense that he never turned up and the teachers and school board were happy to have him gone.

Now Benton was hanging out with Steve and his cronies. He had to admit he felt excited, his heart thumping with the prospect of what might happen.

Whenever they saw someone that they took exception to, they would shout abuse. The victims of these tirades would just hang their heads and quicken their pace. Benton had never felt so empowered.

As they headed into the market place, Joe, the youngest boy in the gang, jumped up and knocked the pay and display sign off its stand. This got cheers from the other boys. Steve rubbed Joe's hood roughly as a show of acceptance. Benton longed to feel that, he wanted to see that his peers were proud of him. Suddenly an idea occurred to him. Adopting the monkey swagger they all seemed to walk with, he sauntered across the market place to St Leonard's church. There, he turned his back on the gang, who were all watching with curious gazes, and began to piss over the church wall.

This gained him not only a cheer, but also a round of rapturous applause.

'Oi!' came a shout from the main road, making Benton freeze in fear midstream. 'What are you doing?'

Benton turned to see a policeman approaching. He wanted to run, he wanted to hide. He looked to the others who were just stood giggling across the market place. As the policeman got closer Benton could see that he wasn't an actual copper, he was one of those Police Community Support Officers. That was bad enough, though. He walked right up to Benton.

'This is a church, you little shit,' the P.C.S.O. said, 'not a bloody urinal.'

'Well, uh, I...' Benton panicked, trying to find the words. He was suddenly aware of Steve walking towards them.

'I can take you in to the station for this,' the P.C.S.O continued, unaware of Steve approaching. 'It's a fine and an A.S.B.O. for you, my son.'

'You can't take him in,' Steve said, bumping into the officer. 'You'd have to call a real pig for that.'

Suddenly the P.C.S.O looked a little concerned. It was clear that he recognised Steve, but then, what police round here didn't?

'Well I can call them to come and get him.'

'You gonna get them to take us all in are ya?' Steve asked, smiling. 'Cos the second you call them on my mate here, we're gonna kick the living shit out of you till they get here. What you reckon their response time will be?'

'A few minutes,' the P.C.S.O. said sheepishly; he knew full well that on a Monday night it would take them far longer than that to get there.

'How much of a beating do you think we could give him in that time?' Steve asked Benton.

'A bad one,' Benton said, trying to hide the fear he was feeling.

'Too right, kidder,' Steve said. 'So why don't you get back in your car and fuck off ya plastic plod bastard.'

The P.C.S.O stood there looking like he wanted to say something, but the look in Steve's eyes told him it was not worth it. He tutted loudly then walked away. The gang began to laugh and jeer him loudly as he walked back to his car.

'Wanker!' Benton shouted. All at once he felt invincible.

Steve put his arm round his shoulders and led him back to the pack.

The next couple of hours were spent wandering the streets, drinking cheap cider and smoking roll ups. They trashed a bus shelter, cracking the perspex cover and graffitiing it with spray paint. Benton had never felt so alive, so full of adrenaline. When they came across another gang of youths, they scared them off, Benton right at the front, threatening to smash one of their faces in. In truth, Benton had never been in so much as a play fight in his whole life. The thought of actual violence terrified him. He knew, though, that with Steve on their side, the other gang wouldn't dare let it turn to actual violence. A year or so back Steve had actually put a kid in a coma in a fight; to this day the kid was a little brain-damaged. Steve had got away with it, though, not enough witnesses, people were too scared of reprisals from the rest of the Murphy clan to testify.

After that, they had gone to the park and messed about on the kids' play area. Benton was, for the first time he could really remember, truly happy. He felt a part of something, something that mattered. He looked at the other guys in the gang. Steve, the leader, bigger than everyone else by about a foot. Joe, the little annoying shit, who made everyone roar with laughter. Tom, Steve's right-hand man, next biggest and toughest. The twins, Jason and Sam, they were the most devious; they were the ones who came up with the best ideas. Then there was Walker, the quiet one. Benton hadn't heard him speak all night, but Steve said he was vicious in a fight. They were the gang, the gang he was now officially part of. They were his friends, and his brothers in arms; together they would tear down the whole fucking town.

'Right,' Steve said.

At the sound of his voice everyone stopped what they were doing and listened intently; he was like a general calling his troops to attention.

'What are we gonna do now?' he said.

There was a quiet mutter, as though no one could think of anything.

'Well,' said Jason, 'I think Bingo will be kicking out on the old people's estate up the road. We could go and rob some grannies for their winnings.'

Benton was appalled by this idea; he had no desire to steal from old ladies. He kept quiet, however, not wanting to lose the respect of his peers. He should have, though, he really should have.

'Not a bad idea,' Steve said. 'I'm a bit short of cash at the minute. Take it easy on them, though, they're only old biddies, no need to rough them up. Threats should be enough.'

And with that they headed up Boston road towards the old people's estate on the edge of town.

At first, it seemed like an utter waste of time. Sure enough, the bingo had finished and the old ladies were walking home, but in big groups. There was no way they'd be able to control that many of them at once, even if they were just old biddies. Not only that, but the estate was small and well lit. One shout from one of the old women and all of the curtains would twitch, and the police would be called. They had escaped a brush with a P.C.S.O. earlier, but Benton doubted they would be able to get out of a brush with a whole squad of coppers.

'Well this was a fucking waste of time,' Sam said, slapping his twin round the head. 'You really are thick as shit sometimes.'

Jason, taking exceptions to the slap, punched Sam in the arm.

'Fuck off, twat!' he yelled. 'It's not like you had any ideas.'

Benton was relieved that the plan had failed, hopefully they would head back to the town centre soon, and that would be the end of this.

'Wait a minute,' Steve said. 'Let's see if there are any stragglers or if any of them look like they're heading off the estate.'

Damn, Benton prayed that none of these things happened. Earlier he had felt elated to be part of the gang, now he was beginning to think he had made a terrible decision. He had always been brought up to respect his elders. His mother had been a home help for years. When he was little and off school she would take him with her. The old dears would fuss over him and give him money or sweets. It had been like having countless grandmothers, all treating him on a daily basis. He wanted no part of this plan.

'I better be getting off home,' he said.

He felt all of their eyes burning into him. They were judging him, seeing that he was not fit to be part of their gang, and if he was not part of the gang, he was a target. He couldn't stand it.

'Only joking,' he said.

The other laughed.

'Good one, kid,' Steve said.

It seemed as if Benton's prayers had been

answered, when after ten minutes they hadn't seen a single viable target. He was sure that the others would get bored of waiting soon, and then they could go and do something else. Then he saw him.

Walking down the street away from the community centre was an old man on his own. He was tall, but very thin, and looked incredibly frail. Benton hoped that the others hadn't seen him, then he saw Sam nudge Steve and nod towards the old man. To make matters worse, the potential victim was wandering towards the path that led alongside the riverbank. There were no streetlights down there and, often, not many people at this time of night. It was too tempting for Steve and the others. Steve nodded.

'Let's follow him,' he commanded, and they set off.

Benton felt sick; it was like there was a washing machine churning away in the pit of his stomach. As they stepped out of the well-lit street and onto the secluded riverside path, it took a while for his eyes to adjust. All he could see up ahead was blackness. He could not see the old man at all. For a few moments his heart raised, perhaps the old man had managed to escape his fate by turning off the path somewhere. Perhaps he had spotted them following him and had decided to hide off the beaten track. Then, as Benton's eyes grew accustomed to the dim lighting, he saw the tall, frail man walking up ahead.

Steve led the way as they headed down the path. Joe followed, yapping at his masters heels like a Jack Russell. Tom and the twins walked together in a line. Benton took up the rear with the still silent Walker. He wanted to do something that would alert the old man to the danger, shout out or give him some kind of signal, but what good would it do? The old man would not be fast enough to get away, and all it would do was make them turn on him, too.

As they neared the old man, he looked back at them. Benton could see he was nervous as he turned his head back around quickly and sped up his pace a little. Steve nodded to Joe, who nodded back and then picked up his pace, running ahead of them after the old man.

'Oi, Mate!' Joe shouted as he closed the gap between him and the poor old man. 'Oi, mate, you dropped this!' Joe was holding up his hand, as if to show the old man something, though Benton knew full well his hand was empty.

The old man took the bait. He turned round and looked at Joe, stopping as he did. At that point, Steve and the rest of the gang charged ahead, leaving only Benton hanging back as much as he could.

The old man saw what was coming and turned and tried to start moving, but it was too late. Little Joe was already upon him and holding his arm. The old man looked terrified.

'Get off me!' he yelled, and then shouted at the top of his lungs. 'Help! Help me!'

He tried to pull away from Joe's grip, but was too frail. He lifted his walking stick as if he was going to hit his assailant with it, but before he could, the others arrived. Tom grabbed the raised walking stick and yanked it out of the old man's hand. For a terrifying moment, Benton thought Tom would use the stick as a weapon against the old man. To his relief, Tom threw the stick into the bushes on the riverbank.

Walker took the old man's free arm. The twins stood off to the side, and then Steve stepped right up to the old man. Benton, as slowly as he was moving, had caught up with them. He just stood off to the side, not wanting to be involved, but too scared to try and stop it.

'Give us your money,' Steve said, his face mere inches away from the old man's.

'Piss off, you hooligan!' the old man said.

Steve smiled and nodded. He turned to look at the rest of the gang. Benton could see the eyes of the others egging him on. Not wanting to be part of it, he looked to the ground. He couldn't stop this from happening, but he was damned if he was going to give Steve his support.

Once he was satisfied that the others were game, Steve turned back to the old man. He pulled back his fist and struck the pensioner, hard in the stomach. The old man bent double, had it not been for Joe and Walker holding his arms he would have fallen to the ground.

Benton felt sick by what he had just seen. He knew now that he did not want the respect of Steve and the gang, they were the worst kind of monsters. It was one thing to feel empowered by frightening those who were weaker than you, but this, this was evil.

As if in response to this thought, Benton heard the twins giggle. He looked over and saw that they found this funny; they were actually enjoying watching a brute like Steve beat up a defenceless old man. Steve put his hand under the old man's chin and lifted his face. Benton, even in the dim light, could see the tears on the man's eyes.

'Give me your fucking money,' Steve said.

'No,' The old man said. His voice sounded rasping as he did his best to hide his pain.

Steve punched the old man in the face. A spray of blood and a wet crunch accompanied the bone in his nose breaking. The man roared in pain like a wounded animal. Benton wanted to cover his ears, close his eyes, and do anything he could to pretend he was somewhere else and not watching this horror unfold, but he could not look away.

The old man slumped to his knees in front of Steve, his arms raised above his head, as Joe and Tom were still holding him. Blood streamed down his face from his ruined nose. He spat out some that had run into his mouth.

'Just give me your money,' Steve repeated.

'I don't have any,' the old man said in a pathetic voice.

'Search him,' Steve said. Walker stepped forward and began to rummage through the old man's pockets. The old man groaned as Walker checked his jacket and trousers. When he was done, Walker looked at Steve and shook his head.

'Fuck it!' Steve shouted. The old man visibly quaked at the anger in his voice.

'What about this?' Joe said, holding the old man's arm out towards Steve, displaying his left hand, and more importantly the thick gold ring on his finger.

Steve grabbed the old man's hand and looked at the ring.

'Is that solid gold?' he asked.

'Please,' the old man spluttered. 'That's my wedding ring; it's all I have left of my wife.'

Steve slapped the old man across the face with the back of his hand.

'Shut up.'

The old man began to sob loudly. Unfazed by the man's anguish, Steve began trying to pull the ring from his finger. It wouldn't come. Steve spat on the old man's finger, using his saliva to try and lubricate the ring free, but still it wouldn't come. Anger on his face, Steve pushed Joe backward, making him release the old man's arm. Steve shoved the man's hand under his face.

'Take it off,' he commanded.

'I can't,' the old man cried out at him. 'I broke that finger years ago, and the ring has been stuck there ever since.'

Suddenly Sam stepped forward, his hand in his pocket.

'I got this Steve-o,' he said grinning.

He pulled a knife out of his pocket. The blade glinted in the scant moonlight. Dread filled Benton's heart. Things were really getting out of hand now.

Steve smiled and held the man's hand up to Sam. The twin with the knife took it in his own and began to cut through the old man's finger. Blood spurted out and the old man howled with pain. It was a noise that surely could have been heard for miles. It seemed to take forever, Sam sawing at the digit. When he had cut all the way down to the bone, he bent the old man's finger back until it snapped and came away from his hand. The old man roared in agony.

'Shut it,' Steve said, kicking the old man hard in the side of the head. Tom let go and the old man crashed to the floor.

'Is he...dead?' Joe asked. Benton couldn't tell if the youngster was nervous or excited from the tone of his voice.

Tom leant down and listened to the old man's chest.

'No, he's breathing,' Tom said.

'We have to get out of here,' Benton finally said. 'Someone would have heard that scream. I bet the police are already on their way.'

Jason, Walker, Tom and Joe all nodded in agreement and started to walk away from the old man. Sam stood there cleaning the blood from his knife on the old man's jacket.

Steve turned to the others.

'Wait,' he said. At the sound of his voice everyone froze. 'This got pretty fucking serious. We can't just leave him here like that'

Benton stopped. Of course, Steve was right, what if no one had called the police? Then the old man would surely die out here in this condition. They had to do something. Benton pulled his phone out of his pocket.

'Yeah, we better call an ambulance for him,' Benton said.

Steve rushed over and slapped the phone out of his hand.

'No, you fucking moron. I meant we have to finish him off.'

At first, Benton couldn't even comprehend what Steve was saying. Then as it dawned on him, he felt an icy shiver run down his spine.

'What?' Benton said. 'You don't mean...?'

'Yes, I mean kill him,' Steve said. 'Think about it. He saw all of our faces. This wasn't just a mugging; Sam cut his fucking finger off.'

To emphasise the point, he waved the severed finger in Benton's face, the thick gold ring still in place.

'If he lives, we'll all go down for this,' Steve said.

'He's right,' Sam agreed. Benton could see now that this twin was not just devious, he was psychotic.

Steve walked over to him and snatched the knife out of his hand.

'We all take a go,' he said, holding the knife up to them. 'That way we know that we're all in it together and no one's gonna grass.'

Benton looked round at the others, hoping for some sign that one of them felt the same way that he did. Alas, it seemed they all agreed with Steve.

Taking the knife in his right hand, Steve headed over to the slumped body of the old man. He raised the glinting blade up and brought it down hard into the man's back. Benton had been expecting the man to scream, or at the very least, to twitch as the blade was buried deep in his body. The old man, though, remained still.

Steve handed the knife to Sam, who gleefully took it. He knelt down besides the old man and rammed the knife, up to the hilt, into his ribs. Benton shuddered as he saw the way that Sam smiled.

Next up was Jason. Though not a cheerful as his twin, he was equally thorough when he stabbed the man in the ribs on the opposite side to his brother. When he was done, Steve took the knife off him and handed it to Joe. The boy, who had been acting so tough all night, now seemed nervous.

'Go on, kid,' Steve said. 'Your turn.'

Joe nodded and walked over to the body. Without looking what he was doing, Joe raised the knife up and drove it down in between the old man's shoulder blades. Benton could have sworn that he saw tears in the younger boy's eyes as he stabbed the old man, but he quickly wiped his face to hide it from the others.

Steve took the knife from Joe and offered it to Tom. The young man who was considered second in command of the gang hesitated. He looked at the knife, then to the bleeding lump on the floor.

'Steve, he's dead,' Tom said. 'It's enough.'

Steve looked calmly at him for a few moments, and then a fire of rage appeared in his eyes. He launched forwards, grabbing Tom by the front of his hoodie with his free hand and holding the knife up to his face with the other.

'I say when it's enough, alright?' Steve screamed. 'All of us are going to cut him, and I swear to God, anyone who doesn't gets the fucking same as he did.'

Tom looked shocked, it was clear that he had never seen Steve behave like this. Sure, Steve had a reputation as a thug, a bully, a hooligan, a petty criminal even, but never had Tom seen that his friend was capable of this. It was too late, though, the old man was dead, and they were all in this together, or they would face the same fate. Steve had graduated to the next level, murderer.

'Fuck's sake,' Tom said snatching the knife out of Steve's hand. He walked over to the old man's body and stuck the knife into his back. He looked back at Steve. 'Alright?'

Steve nodded. Tom shook his head and walked away. As he passed him, he handed the knife to Walker.

The silent youth walked over to the old man's body, though by now Benton suspected the correct term was corpse, and knelt down. He looked up at Steve, their leader nodded.

'You know this is wrong?' Walker said.

Benton was not the only one who was surprised by this; it was clear from all of their expressions that it was a real rarity for him to talk. His voice was for more gentle and eloquent than Benton had expected.

'What?' Steve said. His rage was building again.

'The way you lot have been wildly stabbing this guy,' Walker said. 'If by any chance he was still alive, it was just fucking cruel. This should have been done first.'

Without a second's hesitation, Walker lifted the old man's head up by his hair and dragged the blade across his throat. Then he got up and walked away, handing the knife back to Steve.

Benton's heart sank. He was the only one left, the only one who had not taken a turn. Despite the fact that they knew it was wrong, Joe, Tom and Walker had all done their duty for the gang. Benton, though, had only been a part of the gang for one night, and decided before the saw the old man that he didn't want to be any longer. Now he was faced with the prospect of stabbing a man. Legally he knew he was probably already an accessory to murder, but if he took hold of that knife and stuck it in the old man's corpse, he would feel it emotionally.

'You're up, Nick' Steve said, holding the knife out to him. No one except his mother had called him by his first name since he had started secondary school; he was always just Benton. It was a connection to when they had been little children, when he and Steve had played together, when they had been friends. They had been so close. Yet the monster standing in front of him now bore no resemblance to that small boy who had been his childhood playmate. He did not recognise the creature he had become and wanted nothing to do with him. If this meant Steve killing him, too, so be it, at least he would die with his conscience clear.

'No,' Benton said, with a strength of conviction that he had never had before in his life.

Steve's eyes burned, but he smiled.

'What?' he said, poking his finger in his ears. 'I don't think I heard you properly.'

'You heard me, alright,' Benton said. He was aware that none of the others were moving, he wasn't even sure they were breathing. They just watched on, half of them wishing they had had the nerve to stand up to Steve, the other half wanting to see Steve tear him apart.

'Didn't you hear what I told him?' Steve said, pointing the knife at Tom. 'Anyone who doesn't do their part gets the same as this old fucker.'

'I heard you,' Benton said. 'I'm just not scared of you. There's nothing you can do that's going to make me stab that poor old man, even if it means you killing me.'

'You're too right it means killing you,' Steve said, then took a step closer.

Benton took off running, hoping he could get back to the old people's estate before the others could catch him. Of course, he had forgotten that Sam, the psycho, was stood behind him and to the right. On seeing him turn, Sam jumped left and grabbed him. Benton kicked and tried to get free. Sam was like a spider, though, his grip constantly shifting to be in the best place. Jason ran over and joined in, grabbing Benton on the opposite side to his twin. Together they managed to drag him to the ground. Benton continued trying to fight his way free of the twins, but it was no use.

Steve stepped over and knelt on his chest. His weight was unbearable, Benton felt like he couldn't breathe. Steve leered down at him, his face a mask of menace.

'I warned you, Nick,' he said, putting the knife up to the side of Benton's face. 'I fucking warned you all.'

Steve dragged the blade across Benton's cheek hard. He screamed in pain as it cut at his flesh. Steve pulled the knife away and admired his handy work, as the blood poured from Benton's cheek. He smiled and nodded to himself, like a workman taking pride in a job well done.

'One last chance,' he said. 'Take this knife and stab the old fucker over there, and this is the worst you get.'

Benton gasped for air, the weight of Steve on his chest made him unable to speak. Steve realised and stood up.

'What did you say?' Steve asked.

'I said, go fuck yourself, Steve,' Benton smiled, despite the pain and the fear he was feeling inside, he had stuck to his guns. If he died now, at least he knew he would have died with some dignity.

'You little prick,' Steve said. He moved to kneel down on Benton once more, but something stopped him. A sound. They all heard it, each of them looking around to see which of them had done it. There had been a definite laugh, a low grating sound, like a motor trying to start.

It was clear from all of their faces that none of them had made the sound. Then they heard it again, this time its point of origin was much more obvious. It came from the bloodied corpse of the old man. He laughed again. This time they could see him moving, his body shaking just a little with each laugh.

Sam and Jason loosed their grip on Benton, both of them watching the old man intently. They looked to Steve, but their leader had no more idea what was happening than they did. All of the boys, Benton included, were stood there, staring in disbelief.

'What the fuck?' Steve said.

At this, the old man roared with laughter. He put his hands under himself and pushed him self up onto his knees. Everything about his expression made him look dead, the slack jaw, the glazed eyes, and yet he was moving. He got to his feet and turned to face them. Without his mouth moving a voice came from him. It was not the voice they had heard earlier; this one was darker, and stronger.

'Nice work, boys,' the corpse said. 'But crimes like this don't go unpunished.'

They were all too terrified to move. Every fibre of Benton's being was screaming at him to run, and not look back. Yet he couldn't, he could not look away from what he was witnessing.

The old man reached up with his hands to the gaping wound on his neck that Walker had inflicted. He placed one hand below the wound, and one above, and then slowly slid his fingertips into the bleeding gash. In what was like a grotesque parody of one of the mask scenes in *Mission Impossible*, the old man began to tear the skin off his head. When the flesh mask was removed, they saw his face, his true face, the one that had been hiding below the surface all along. It was perfect, flawless. It reminded Benton of a statue carved in marble, only it was red. Not from the blood, either, his skin was bright red. His teeth were gleaming white, but all filed to sharp points. His eyes glowed with fire, and his long black hair cascaded back in sweeping waves. Protruding from his forehead were two small but clearly visible horns.

He threw off his jacket and bent forward. Two enormous, skeletal looking wings ripped out of his shoulder blades.

'Pleased to meet you, boys,' the thing said with a wry smile. 'Hope you guess my name.'

He looked around their terrified faces. Each of them stood there with their mouths open, unable to look away.

'I love the smell of fear,' the thing said. He slowly raised his hand and pointed straight at Benton.

Benton wanted to scream, but no sound would come from him.

'You,' the thing said, still pointing at him. 'You don't belong here. Go, now, and don't look back.'

Suddenly Benton was able to move again, he turned to run. He took one last look at the other boys.

Their eyes begged him for help, but he had none to give. He set off back up the path along the riverbank.

'Oh, Benton?' The thing said after him. Benton stopped in his tracks and looked back. 'Stay out of trouble, or we might meet again.'

Benton ran, not knowing what hell awaited the others, just knowing that 'Hell' was exactly the right word. As he made his way quickly along the path, he could hear the tortured screams and cries and pitiful begging of the other boys, but he didn't look back. From now on, he was staying away from trouble, far, far away.

THE HOUSE BY THE MARSH

I first laid eyes on the house by the marsh when I was fifteen years old. At that time, my family lived in a village called Wyberton, which was just outside the market town of Boston in Lincolnshire. It was a fairly dull place to be a teenager, but I was lucky enough to have a large group of friends. We would spend our time flitting between each other's houses, hanging around the local SPAR shop, or just roaming the streets.

Sometimes, usually in the summer when the weather was good, we would wander across the A16, the road that had split the village in two, and head out into the countryside. We would walk past the church and the graveyard and down the narrow winding roads that led to the marsh.

There was a network of these single lane roads, all of which seemed to converge at the marsh. I thought that we had walked all of them over the years, but it turned out I was mistaken.

It was a warm May evening when we had set off from my friend Wayne's house. He was the only one of us that lived on that side of the main road. That night there were seven of us hanging around in his bedroom. There was myself; my best friend Rob; Danny, the joker of the group; Rob's sister Zara and her friends Lizzie and Wendy; and of course, Wayne himself.

We had grown bored of listening to music and drinking too-warm bottles of cheap French beer. We thought about heading to the shop or maybe paying a call on another of our friends, but we were all skint and couldn't think of anyone who would be home that night. Instead, we made the decision to walk out towards the marsh. If nothing else did, this would always keep us entertained.

It was around seven in the evening as we left Wayne's house. The sky had taken on that darkening grey colour of a spring evening, but the air was still warm. The group of us set out down Wayne's road, passing the familiar landmarks on our way. First, we came to the bridge that went over a small stream. As always, Danny would try and pick Rob up to throw him into the stream, and as always Rob would fight his way free of Danny's grip. He may have been small, but Rob was as slippery as a fish when you tried to get hold of him.

Then we turned down the road that led to the church. Even back then I always thought it was a beautiful little church. It seemed secluded and peaceful, tucked away from the main road, its churchyard surrounded by trees. It had a little graveyard around it, with crumbling old tombstones you could barely read anymore.

A little further down the road was the more modern cemetery; this was hidden behind a large, red brick wall and was accessible only through a wrought iron gate. Despite the fact that it was newer and tidier, this was the one that freaked us out the most. In there you could clearly see the names and dates of deaths and some of them were painfully close to home.

We carried on walking down the lane until we passed the last row of houses, then there was nothing around us but fields on either side of the road. The sun had sunk a little lower in the sky by this point, engulfing the bottom of the vast sky in shades of orange, pink and red. Due to the flat nature of most of

Lincolnshire, you always got these massive skies. With nothing to block them, they were often breathtaking, and this was no exception.

As we walked the open country lanes, we laughed and joked, talked about school and all the random crap that went with it. Time always seemed to pass slowly on those walks, after all, we were young and without a care in the world, except for those we created for ourselves.

The air got a little cooler once we were out in the open. With nothing to stop it for miles around, the wind was usually quite strong. Out of nowhere there was a clap of thunder, the skies darkened significantly and then the heavens opened with a ferocity I had never seen before, nor have I seen since. The rain was so heavy that we could barely see. We ran blindly for an open barn in the field to our right, soaked to the skin and looking a rather sorry state.

The storm only lasted a few minutes, but made the earth soggy in the field. The girls had enough; when the rain subsided, they decided that they were going home. We decided, though, that as we could not feasibly get any wetter we may as well carry on walking out to the marsh.

After the girls had left us, Wayne pointed out the road opposite the one they had taken.

'I bet that goes back to the church, too,' he said with mischievous glee. 'We could double back there and scare the shit out of them by jumping out of the graveyard.'

The general opinion amongst the rest of us was that this was quite possibly the greatest idea that Wayne had ever had. We hurried out of the field and went quickly up the other road, not running, but wanting to gain enough ground to get there ahead of the girls. The only problem was that the road suddenly took a swing to the left around a hairpin bend. Instead of heading for the church we were now back heading for the marsh. It was too late now to find another way back in time to scare them, so we decided to follow the road to its end.

Like all of the other roads we used to walk around there, this one was narrow and winding. Unlike the others, though, it was tree-lined most of the way down. Tangled branches reached for each other above our heads. There was something creepy and beautiful about it all at the same time.

As we got nearer the marsh, the smell of the sea became more apparent. Some people didn't like the smell, but I always found it refreshing. The road veered off to the right, another hairpin bend. As I would find out a few years later, this road was a nightmare to drive unless you knew it well.

One thing that struck me as odd, even that first time walking down there, was there were no houses. The other roads were desolate yes, but there was always the odd home here and there, but this one was empty for miles. As the bank that ran along the marsh came into view on our left, we saw the house. It stood there alone, up ahead on the right. Even from that distance it looked wrong, out of proportion in some way. It looked like it had been a small house originally and then extended badly, to create something that just didn't look right.

Something about the place had stopped us all in our tracks without one of us saying a word. I looked to my friends; each of them was staring towards the house with an expression of intrigue and trepidation on their faces.

'That's a creepy looking place,' Danny said, finally breaking the silence that had befallen us.

'Too right,' Wayne seconded.

'Let's get a closer look,' I said.

'Yeah,' Rob replied.

At this stage, I should point out that Rob and I were obsessed with horror movies and ghost stories. They scared us stupid sometimes, but nevertheless we were thrilled at the idea of exploring such a foreboding looking place.

The other two were a little more apprehensive, though they tried not to show it, not wanting to appear like cowards compared to us. So, the four of us continued down the road towards the house.

As we got closer, it became clear that the house was derelict. The windows and door were boarded up with slats with gaps in between. There were black marks above the front door and windows, evidence of a fire at some point. The garden was a state, it was overgrown, but all of the plants looked brown and dead. Its state of disrepair made it look even more ominous. As we approached the short fence that surrounded the property, a gust of cold wind blew across our faces, strong enough to bring tears to our eyes.

I felt something in the pit of my stomach, a kind of dragging sensation that made me feel queasy. I knew what had caused the feeling. It was the house. It was my body telling me to leave as the house tried to pull me towards it. I looked to the others for some sign that they were experiencing it, too. Though they looked a little nervous, I could see that none of them were having the physical reaction to the house that I was.

'It's burnt out,' Rob said as we looked towards the house.

'Yeah, but it doesn't look like it was a bad fire,' Danny, whose father was a fireman, said. 'Looks like a small fire to have done that.'

'Oh, God,' Wayne said. 'I know what this is. It's the paedo's house!'

We all looked at him, confused. He, in turn, looked back at us for some recognition and saw none. We had no idea what he was talking about. Wayne was often in possession of information about local goings on that we were not because he had an older brother who knew the area well. I was the youngest in my family and had two older brothers, though we had only moved to the area when I was twelve, so my brothers didn't grow up round here or go to school here. Rob and Danny were both the eldest in their families.

'It was about eight years ago, I think,' Wayne began to explain. 'They found out some kiddie fiddler was living out here. He had been abusing kids for ages. The police didn't have enough evidence to convict him so they let him go. Some of the parents of the kids he'd messed with didn't like it, so they came down here to burn his house down.'

So far, we were all pretty convinced that Wayne was in fact just repeating the origin story of Freddy Krueger, especially as we were all big fans of the *Nightmare on Elm Street* films at the time.

'Thing is, the police were watching the house so they got the fire brigade here before the fire could really take hold. Your dad might have been one of them,' he said to Danny.

'Maybe,' Danny said, knowing that his father would never tell them about actual fires he'd been to, just the dangers of fire.

'Anyway,' Wayne continued. 'When they went in to fight the fire, they found the paedo hanging in the hallway, he'd killed himself.'

I got a chill down my neck as he said this. Six months earlier, unbeknownst to any of them, I had tried to hang myself. I wouldn't find out for many years, but I was suffering from bipolar disorder. Sometimes I just felt like life was not worth living, for no reason. I had a happy home, a family who loved me, friends who were great, yet still there were these dark periods where nothing seemed to make me feel better.

'They say that if you go and peek through the board on the doorway, you can still see him hanging there, reaching out to touch whatever kid dares to look.'

'Bollocks,' Rob said.

'No, my brother told me one of his mates saw him, then went crazy,' Wayne said.

'Also bollocks,' I added.

'Well why don't you go and look,' Wayne said.

I had no good answer, accept that I was scared to. I, who was obsessed with the supernatural and horror films, was too scared to go and look through a boarded up door on a spooky house. It was not to do with Wayne's, more than likely false, story. It was because of the way that looking at the house made me feel. The queasiness and the pulling sensation were too much for me to take.

'I will,' said Danny, in an uncharacteristically brave move.

He hopped over the short fence and made his way slowly through the decaying plants of the garden. I wanted to scream at him not to go, but all that would have achieved was to make the others mock me for being a coward.

Danny looked back at us as he approached the door. He seemed so far away from us, from the safety of the group, I imagined a hand coming through the boards on the door and pulling him into the blackness of the house.

He waved at us and grinned before kneeling down to look through a gap in the boards. I could hear my own heartbeat in my ears; it felt quicker than it should have. We all stood in silence as Danny looked into the house, into the abyss. It felt like forever that he knelt there. Time seemed to stop. The breeze that was ever present down near the marsh was gone, there was no sound of birds or insects or even the rumble of distant traffic on the A16. All that I could hear was the thump of my own heart, and my own breathing.

'Fuck this,' Danny screamed getting up and running back across the garden. In the style of true childhood friends, we did not wait for him to reach us, instead we ran full pelt back up the road, and around the hairpin bend. We did not stop for him to catch up with us until the house was well out of sight. Danny came running up to us panting. His face was whiter than I'd ever seen anyone look. His eyes were wide. He looked terrified.

'What did you see?' Rob asked.

'Nothing,' Danny said, his voice sounding strange and distant.

'You must have seen something,' I said. 'You look scared.'

Danny barged past us and headed up the road, back towards Wyberton. He looked back at us.

'I don't want to talk about it,' he said. 'I just want to go home.'

Rob, Wayne and I looked at each other, then headed off down the road after him. We walked home in silence.

The years went by and things changed. Rob went off to university in Nottingham, Wayne joined the Army, and Danny went off the rails. He got in with a bad crowd and started stealing and doing drugs. I stayed where I was and studied for my degree at the local college. Rob and I still saw each other as often as possible, but rarely did we see the others. That night, and the house, faded into the dark recesses of my memory. I continued to suffer, undiagnosed, with bipolar disorder. There were some dark times for me over those years. Self-harm was the big thing, not in the attention seeking way that so many people do, no, I hid it carefully for years. For me it was all about the sense of relief cutting gave me. I was in control of it and it seemed to release all of the pressure and negativity that built up in my mind. Several times, I ended up in hospital being stitched after cutting too deep, yet still I always found an excuse to explain it away as an accident, and not as something I has deliberately done to myself.

My next encounter with the house by the marsh came while I was studying for my degree in media studies. We had been assigned a photography project based on the theme of decay. The mention of that word brought the house screaming back into my head. I was still wary of the idea of going back there, but I told myself that we had just been scared kids, messing around. Danny was a twat, as he had proved since, and was probably just messing around. I decided to go back and take some photos of the house for my project.

It was a lovely, warm and sunny day in early June when I drove back out there. I remember the time well as a friend of mine from college, Jane, had gone missing a few weeks prior. It had been so long, five years in fact, since I had last been to the house that it took me a few attempts to find the right road. I forgot about, and nearly lost control of the car going around, that final hairpin bend. I felt a chill as the house loomed into view. Even in the bright summer sun it looked dark. It was as though darkness clung to the place, refusing to let it into the light. I pulled up across the road and stepped outside, trying to shake off my trepidation, telling myself it was nothing but a silly childhood memory. I picked up the college's Pentax SLR camera I had borrowed to take the shots. It was loaded with a roll of black and white film, with 24 shots. I had taken eight shots earlier at the old churchyard at Wyberton, on my way here. I had remembered those crumbling gravestones and thought they would fit in perfectly with the theme of decay.

I took a few shots of the house from the, what I felt, relative safety of the road. I took a few wide shots, though I knew I would probably not use these. Then I got down on the ground and took a shot through the rusting fence and overgrown garden. Through the view finder of the camera, the house looked like a beast in the undergrowth, waiting to pounce. I knew the shot I wanted, though, and it would require me to get closer to the house than I was. I took a deep breath to steady my nerves. Once again I heard the sound of my own heartbeat, thumping in my ear.

I stepped over the fence and into the jungle of dead plants that was the garden. I instantly felt light-headed and queasy. I had once suffered from vertigo, and that is the only sensation I could liken it to. I wanted to turn around and jump back over the fence, to get in my car and leave the place, never to return. Yet I needed this photo, my overall grades had been slipping a little due to one of my low periods so I knew I had to pull something special out of the bag for this project in order to progress to my final year.

I shook off the feeling and marched towards the house. I went to the large window on the left of the house. It was boarded up, but there were plenty of gaps through which I could get the shots. I saw that the glass was completely gone from the window. I was going to be sticking the lens into the house. I imagined it being pulled away from me by an unseen force. I pushed this image out of my mind.

There was a smell; it was prevalent even on the road, but was stronger near the house. It was unlike anything I had smelled before, except maybe when one of my cuts had got infected. It had oozed a sticky brown substance that smelt like death. That was what the house smelled of, infection and death.

I quickly snapped a few shots blind. I was unwilling to look through the viewfinder for fear of what might be looking back at me. I hoped they would be in focus.

Next, I moved to the door. This was the shot I wanted, through the gaps in the boards, into the open doorway. The same view my old friend Danny had got all those years ago. Would I see whatever it was that he had seen? I wanted this shot to be perfect, so once I had the lens through the gap, I knelt down and looked through the viewfinder. It was dark inside and I could not make much out. I tried to find something to focus on, and in the end, I spotted an old plant pot down toward the end of the hallway. I used this as my focal point, set up my aperture and exposure time, I set it for the flash knowing that without it I would see nothing.

I paused for a second, thinking I heard movement from inside. I listened intently, but there was nothing. I pressed the button on the camera and the flash illuminated the inside of the hallway for a split second. It was long enough for me to register a figure hanging in the hallway, by the stairs, an area that had been completely hidden in shadow. It was the spirit of the paedophile who had committed suicide in the house. I scrambled away from the door on my hands and knees almost leaving the camera behind. I got up and ran back to the car. I drove back home, my nerves shredded. Had I seen a ghost? I told myself that it was not possible, it was my imagination. Of course when I developed the film I would know for sure.

I used up the rest of the film on some gnarled driftwood, and a burnt out car. It was a few days before I got round to developing the film. By that time I had convinced myself that I hadn't seen anything, that it had just been a product of my overactive imagination. I was sure that when the film was developed and the photographs printed, they would reveal nothing but an empty, ruined old house.

I am not afraid of the dark, never have been. In fact, I have always kind of enjoyed it in a strange way. So, for me, standing in the pitch black studio while developing film was never usually a problem. That day however, with the memory of the house and the knowledge that soon my worst fears would be either confirmed or disproved, I felt more uncomfortable than I had in my entire life. I listened to the clock on the wall slowly tick by the seconds as I tried to load the spool of film into the developing canister. I became convinced I was not alone. It felt as though there was someone else in the room with me, standing behind me. I could feel breath on my neck, it made the little hairs rise. I quickly finished loading the film and flicked on the light. Of course, there was no one in there. How could there have been? I waited for the film to develop and then set it to dry. Usually I would have waited in the developing room while this happened. That day, though, after that feeling of not being alone, I needed to get out, see the sunlight, and other people.

I went outside for twenty minutes. I spoke with a few friends and smoked a few cigarettes before returning to collect my film and prepare it for enlarging. The film was dry so I cut it into manageable strips. I went into the enlarging room and used a lightbox to examine the negatives. I could not believe or explain what I saw. All of the photos taken before I went to the house and the ones taken in the churchyard were fine. All of the ones taken after—the driftwood and the burnt out car—were also perfect, but every single photograph taken at the house was fogged out completely. Nothing was visible at all. It was as though the house had not wanted me to take the pictures. I could not think of any reason this would have occurred. If some light had gotten to the film, all of the photographs would have been corrupted, not just these select few.

I considered going back with another camera and fresh film and trying again, but I saw the fogged out images and the feeling of someone being in the developing room with me as a warning I was best off not to ignore.

A few weeks passed by, and the incident with the house was put to the back of my mind. There were other things to concentrate on, my slipping grades for one. I was in serious danger of not passing my second year. Also, there was the low I had sunken into. I was finding it hard to get out of bed most days and not sleeping at nights. Then, of course, there was the worrying about my missing friend Jane. She was not the only one. Two other girls from the area were missing, one I didn't know and one who I had met briefly in passing. The rumour mill was flying with speculation that Boston had its first serial killer.

When the news broke that the bodies had been found, I was only half-surprised to hear that they had been discovered in that house, the one by the marsh, the one that had been haunting me for years. The girls had been sexually assaulted and killed, their bodies left in the house to decay. They had been there some time.

My stomach turned as I realised that this was what I had smelt that day I went to take the photographs. I had been nosing through the windows and door whilst my friend and two other young women were rotting inside the house.

The real shock came when they announced that the killer had sent a letter to the police telling them what he had done and where they would find the bodies. He offered an apology to the families in this letter and said that he had not been able to stop himself. He had hung himself in the house.

The figure hanging in the hallway I had seen as the flash of my camera went off had not only been real, but had been the body of a murderer. If only I had thought about the smell and not been convinced what I had seen had been an illusion at best, or something supernatural at worst, then maybe I would have called the police and the bodies would have been discovered sooner. It would not have helped the girls, they were already dead, but maybe the suffering of not knowing would have been relieved sooner for their families.

The next day the police put out a statement naming the killer. It was my old school friend Danny. Danny the class joker, Danny the gentle giant, Danny who had stared into that house and seen something so horrendous it had sent him running in fear and left him unable to tell anyone about it. I had always had the feeling that the night he looked into the house had something to do with him going off the rails. He was not the sort of person I would have seen as a druggy or criminal up to that point. Now I wondered if it was also responsible for what he had done to those young women. If not, then why had he chosen that house?

Naturally, there was a very poor turnout for Danny's funeral, people generally don't want to go and mourn multiple murderers. Yet due to that sacred bond of childhood friendship, I was in attendance, as were Rob and Wayne. The three of us sat at the back of the church, leaving a gap between us and the few members of his family who had shown up. I felt sorry for the vicar, trying to find nice words to say about a young man he obviously considered to be a monster.

After the service, the three of slunk away to a nearby pub. It had been a long time since we had seen Wayne. He was doing well in the army. He planned to serve another eight years and then leave. He also informed us that he was getting married at the end of the year; he would have invited us but it was a small service for family only. He showed us a photograph of his little twin girls Iris and Emma. They were beautiful, eight months old and full of life apparently.

Wayne left early to go and meet his fiancée and kids. Rob and I remained in the pub.

'It's fucked up,' Rob said. 'I mean, I know that Danny had turned into a bit of a twat, but murder?'

I took a sip of my drink and nodded.

'Why do you think he did it?' Rob asked me.

'Why do you think?' I replied. 'Why choose that house? It's all down to whatever he saw that night when we were fifteen.'

'Some one should buy that place,' he said, staring off into the distance, 'and level it to the fucking ground.'

Four years later, that is exactly what happened. I was sat at home one day reading a book when my doorbell rang. I answered it to find Rob stood on my doorstep in one of his now trademark, designer business suits.

After leaving university Rob had made a small fortune by developing some sort of all singing, all dancing, data processing software that I did not fully understand. All I knew was that Rob was now the richest man I knew and still my best friend.

'What are you doing here?' I said, confused by his sudden appearance. Usually he gave me three weeks notice of when he was home, so busy was his schedule.

'Get some fucking shoes on,' he said, looking down at my mismatched socks. Then he grinned. 'I've got something to show you.'

I pulled on my Converse and tatty old leather jacket and got into the passenger side of Rob's brand new, drop top Mercedes. Never had I looked or felt more out of place than I did in that car as we drove through Wyberton. We crossed the A16 and drove past the church. I was still unaware of our destination at that point, but when we turned onto that familiar tree-lined road, my heart sank.

'Where are we going?' I said nervously.

'You'll see,' Rob said with a wry smile.

I sank down in my seat, not wanting to be heading where we were heading.

As we turned that last hairpin bend, I looked up expecting to see that damned house staring back at me, like a monster from a fairy tale. To my amazement, though, I saw nothing. The house was gone.

'What the fuck?' I asked sitting up.

Rob laughed out loud. This was the reaction he was hoping I would give.

'You bought it, didn't you?' I said, shaking my head. 'You bought that fucking hellhole?'

'I did, indeed,' he said with a beaming smile, 'and as of nine o'clock this morning that house ceased to exist. I told you years ago that someone should buy the place and level it to the ground.'

'Yes but, I didn't think you meant you,' I said.

'I know, neither did I,' he said, still grinning like the Cheshire cat. 'Then I got rich, and I couldn't get the place out of my head.'

I looked at him, scrutinised him, then I saw it in his eyes.

'You came back here, didn't you?' I said. 'You came back and looked through that fucking door.'

He nodded.

'When?' I asked. I was worried now, what if his obsession led to the horrible things that Danny's had?

'That night after Danny's funeral,' he said. 'You went home half cut, and I went for a walk. I don't know why, but I ended up here. I stood there shouting abuse at the house, at Danny, at God even. Then I decided I was going to look in that door.'

'You stupid tit,' I said. 'After what happened to Danny?'

He looked at me.

'You did it, too,' he said. 'You told me you took a picture through the door.'

'That was before I knew what Danny had done,' I said in my defense.

'You didn't see anything, did you?' he said.

I had lied and told him that I had not seen anything, how was I supposed to tell him that I had seen a hanging figure and been so scared I ran away, only to then find out that it was the corpse of one of our closest school friends.

'No,' I lied again. 'Of course not. Did you?'

Rob shook his head but refused to look me in the eyes. I knew in my gut that he was also lying. I did not know what power the house had held over us, but it had been there in the back of all of our minds since that first time we saw the place.

Now it was gone. We stepped out of the car and surveyed the now empty plot. Everything was gone, the fence, the overgrown garden and the house itself. The crew that Rob had hired for the demolition had taken away all the debris and turned over the earth. All that remained was a large square of fresh brown dirt.

I felt a sense of relief, surely now whatever curse we had brought upon ourselves was over.

'So what are you planning to do with the land?' I asked as we stood there looking at the empty space the house used to occupy. 'Selling it on?'

Rob shrugged.

'At some point probably. Though I might build a new house there first. Make a much better profit.'

'Is that a good idea?' I said

'It's gone, Chris,' Rob said. 'It's over, the house is gone. Time to start afresh. What better way than building a new house here?'

I looked at him. I knew him well enough to know that when he had his mind set on something it was almost impossible to convince him otherwise, it was the personality trait that had made him the wealthy young man that stood before me now.

'Promise me one thing,' I said, looking back out across the fresh earth.

'What?' he said.

'You won't live here, you won't ever come back here,' I said. 'I think the only way that we can truly end this is if we all stay away.'

'Sure thing,' he said. 'I have no intention of living here myself.'

It was a lie. I later became sure that even that day as we looked at the place the house had stood, that Rob knew full well the house he was building was for him and his wife. It took months for me to find out. Rob avoided all contact with me, as far as I was aware he was still living in the city running his software company. Little did I know that once again we were living in the same postcode, that Rob had sold his company and retired at the grand old age of twenty-six.

It was early December when I found out. It was late night shopping in Boston, the streets lit up with Christmas lights and the smell of roast chestnuts clinging to the air. I walked through the hustle and bustle of the crowds, minding my own business. My bipolar disorder had finally been diagnosed. After years of wondering what the hell was wrong with me, I finally had a name. This was actually a great relief, knowing that my mood swings and erratic behaviour were actually a symptom of a medical condition. I had new medication and for the first time in what felt like forever, I felt good about myself.

I was just walking past Oldrids, the town's very own department store, when I saw Lucy, Rob's wife, coming towards me. She was laden down with so many shopping bags that I rushed to help her. She looked pleased to see me and greeted me with a kiss on the cheek.

'It's so good to see you,' she said as I lightened her load.

'You, too,' I said. I walked her to the multi storey car park behind Oldrids, carrying most of the bags.

'How's Rob?' I asked.

'He's good,' she said, but there was something in her tone of voice that concerned me. She must have picked up on it. 'No, really, he's fine. I think he's just having some trouble adapting to all the free time now he's sold the company.'

This was the first I had heard of this. I was shocked, Rob and I were never in constant contact, but I was sure he would have told me some major news like that.

'He what?' I said.

'He sold the company, about six months ago, didn't he tell you?' Now she looked concerned. I neither wanted to cause Lucy any undue distress, nor get my best friend in trouble with his wife.

'Oh, yes,' I lied. 'Of course he did. Sorry it's these new meds they've given me, they're playing havoc with my memory.'

She smiled. Lucy had always been one of the most understanding people about my mood swings, more so than her husband if I was honest.

'You poor thing,' she said, putting a gentle hand on my arm. 'Is that why you haven't been round to see the house yet?'

I knew instantly what house she meant. I knew why I had not heard from Rob in months, and I knew why he had not told me about selling the company. He had broken his promise to me; he had done the one thing he had told me he wouldn't. He had built a new house by the marsh and he was living there.

'You say he's having trouble adjusting?' I said. 'In what way?'

'Oh it's nothing, really,' she said. 'He's just drinking a little more than usual, and he's moody some times, but I'm sure it will get better soon.'

I nodded and we continued walking to the car park. There was a silence between us, one that was not uncomfortable, but it was there.

When we reached the car, I loaded the bags into the boot for her. She thanked me.

'We're having a little Christmas party next week, it would be great if you could make it,' she said. 'It's on Friday night.'

'Damn I have to work,' I lied. There was no way in hell I was going to set foot in that house. 'Get Rob to call me, though, I've not heard from him in a while.'

She told me that she would pass the message on, and then we parted.

I never did hear from Rob and never would again. The following week at his and Lucy's Christmas party, Rob went mad. He shot seven people, killing six of them including Lucy, before turning the gun on himself. The survivors told how Rob had not seemed himself all night, he was distant and quiet, not at all like the Rob I knew. They also explained that he looked disheveled, his clothes creased and his hair a mess, and needing a shave. Rob prided himself on his appearance, and since he had the money to get the best of everything, he always looked good. The friends of his who had survived that night explained that Lucy kept apologising for him whenever he left the room, saying he had been a little under the weather. They said that Lucy herself looked tired, as though she had not been sleeping well. When questioned, she had said that Rob hadn't been sleeping well and been wandering the house at all hours and it had affected her sleeping.

After everyone had eaten, except Rob who apparently just sat there moving the food around his plate, Rob got up and left the room. The stress was beginning to show on Lucy they said, who started crying. While most of the guests tried to comfort Lucy, her brother, Niles, went to see what the hell Rob was playing at.

According to the survivors, Niles had only been gone a few minutes when they heard the first shot, a deafening bang that made them all jump. None of them thought it was a gunshot, though, why would they? Niles was the first to die, shot in the head at close range with 9 mm pistol. God knows where Rob had gotten the gun, but those things aren't hard to find when you have the money. Rob then proceeded back to the dining room, where he began to fire off rounds in all directions. He shot his dear wife, Lucy, three times in the chest. When he ran out of ammo, he slipped in another magazine and continued firing on the guests who were all running around trying to escape him. When he was down to the last round, he turned the gun on himself. One survivor said that his last words were 'You win.'

None of the guests, nor the police, nor anyone else knew the meaning of those final words Rob uttered, no one except me that is. I knew all too well what he meant, the house had won, it had beaten him. The old house may have been destroyed, but whatever evil it was that lingered there was in the very earth itself.

The house was sold to pay compensation to all of those who had been injured and those who had lost family in Rob's killing spree. It was no surprise to me that it was soon boarded up, the place was now involved in so many hideous crimes and deaths that surely no one would want to live there again.

I became ever more obsessed with the house by the marsh, at least twice a week I would drive down there, just to make sure that it was still all boarded up and secure. Having been one myself, I knew full well what the kids round here were like. A boarded up house is tempting for teenagers, they liked to try and get in, either looking for ghosts or just to trash the place. Not that I cared if they wrecked the place, I just didn't want anyone going in there for their own safety. There was something about having direct contact with the place that infected you with its darkness. It had happened to both Danny and Rob, and I felt it myself, every time I went down there. It was a pulling sensation in the pit of my stomach, a desire in my head to just take a quick look inside, but I fought it, knowing that if I entered the house once it would gradually draw me in, corrupting me as it had my friends.

On my thirtieth birthday, I had a surprise phone call from Wayne, asking me if I wanted to go out for a celebratory drink. I had only spoken to Wayne twice since Danny's funeral, and one of those times was at Rob's. I agreed to go and meet him, though. I had been feeling a little low and thought that a drink with one of my oldest friends might pick me up.

It started as a pleasant afternoon. We went into town to the gastro pub by the river and sat there catching up. Wayne said that he only had a few more months left in the army and that he and his family would be moving back to the area. He showed me pictures of the girls, who were now eight years old and absolutely beautiful. I told him how much I envied him, his wife, his kids, his place in life. I had drifted along from one relationship to another, most of them toxic from the start. It seemed that no one knew how to deal with my condition, and expecting them to do so was unfair on my part. Career wise I had drifted from one thing to another, never lasting more than a year, usually a lot less. I started every job with great enthusiasm, but then a low period would hit, and I would lose all interest in everything. The jobs I didn't get fired from, I quit.

We talked about the old days and, of course, about Danny and Rob, not the murderers they became in adulthood, but the kids we had known. These were happy memories, which had us both crying with laughter.

'I just can't understand how they turned out the way they did,' Wayne said, souring the mood. 'Especially not Rob, he was always so together.'

'Yeah, I know,' I said.

I didn't know whether to tell him my theory, that something dark and twisted had got inside us when we all looked into that house. Would he understand? He had seen the house, and been as afraid of it as we had, but would he believe such a wild story, especially from a man who had spent the last four years on antipsychotic drugs?

'Sometimes I wonder if it was that old house by the marsh,' Wayne said, as though reading my thoughts. I looked at him open mouthed, shocked that he had made that connection as well.

'What makes you say that?' I asked, not wanting to give away too much too soon.

'Sometimes I dream about that house. I know it's long gone now, Rob saw to that, but in my dreams it's still there.'

'In a way I think it is,' I said. 'It just looks different now.'

'You remember that night we first found the place?' Wayne asked.

'Like it was yesterday,' I said.

'I think something got hold of Danny when he looked through that crack in the door. Something that made him do those things to those girls.'

I couldn't believe that Wayne, who had been away for so long, had the exact same theory as me.

'Then Rob looked in there, that night after Danny's funeral,' Wayne continued.

'How did you know about that?' I asked, shocked. I had only learned that from Rob after the house was destroyed.

'I was with him,' Wayne said.

'What?'

'He rang me up, half cut, saying you had gone home cos you couldn't handle your booze, and that he was too drunk to drive, so he needed a lift,' he explained. 'At first I thought he just meant a lift home, but he soon told me where he wanted to go.'

I put my head in my hands, then looked up at Wayne.

'Did you look through the crack in door, too?' I asked.

Wayne nodded.

'What did you see?' I asked him, hoping just once to get a straight, honest answer to that question.

'Nothing,' he said. I couldn't tell if he was lying or not. 'Something freaked Rob out, though, he wouldn't tell me anything.'

'So we've all looked into that house,' I said. 'It keeps on pulling us back, one at a time and making us do evil things.'

Wayne and I went our separate ways not long after that conversation. I was troubled, the thought that none of us were safe played heavily on my mind. I began to check the house everyday. Some nights I even slept in my car outside it, just to make sure that no one, especially Wayne, went anywhere near it.

A few months later, I was woken by the sound of a car pulling up behind mine outside the house. My neck was stiff from sleeping in the car and I felt groggy. What sleep I had managed was uncomfortable and filled with dark dreams. I looked in my rearview mirror and saw a familiar face getting out of the car behind. It was Lance Jones, another old school friend. He was one of the most successful local estate agents.

I got out of the car and stretched my aching legs. It was nine in the morning and the sun was shining, casting a golden haze over the fields and hedgerows around me. I looked at the house and saw that still it looked dark, shadows clung to it as though they were painted on. I turned and waved at Lance, he looked confused.

'Alright, Chris?' he said. 'What are you doing out here?'

I walked over and shook his hand.

'I just went for a drive last night, and felt tired so I pulled over, must have slept all night,' I lied.

'Christ, I bet you're a bit stiff this morning then?' he said, walking over to the boot of his car.

'A little,' I replied. 'What brings you out here?'

He didn't need to answer when I saw him pull the new sign out of the boot. It clearly said SOLD, in big bold letters. I felt for a second like I was going to faint, all of the energy left me, my legs buckled and I had to lean against the car to stop from falling. Lance didn't notice, he was too busy getting the sign out of the boot.

'I've finally managed to sell the place,' he said with a beaming grin. 'Not for anywhere near what it's worth, but still it's a commission, and it means the place is finally off my hands.'

I wanted to punch him in his stupid, smug, beaming face. I wanted to break his nose and scream at him, ask him if he had any idea what he had done. I controlled myself, not allowing myself to give in to the darkness inside me; that was exactly what the house wanted. I could feel it watching me, I could almost hear its voice whispering in my ear, telling me to hit him, beat him, kill him. I pushed the thought away.

'How did you manage it?' I said. 'I mean aren't you supposed to tell people about things like what happened here?'

Lance beamed again.

'I didn't have to,' he said. 'He knew all about it.'

A mix of realisation and dread hit me hard. I didn't have to ask him, I knew now who had bought the house, I just wanted to hear it from his lips.

'Who bought it?' I asked.

'I'm not really supposed to give out that information,' he said. 'But he'll tell you himself, I'm sure. It now belongs to Wayne Cooper.'

I went home and called Wayne. I asked him if he was back in town. He said that he was staying at his mum's with the girls while his wife finalised the sale of her house in Yorkshire. I didn't ask him about the house by the marsh, nor did he tell me his news about buying it. I asked him if he was free later for a drink. He said that he could fit me in for a few hours.

We met up at the same pub we had gone to when we had spoken last. As I approached the bar, I was shocked at his appearance. He was stood there waiting for me, his hair was longer than I'd seen it since we left school, and more unkempt than I'd ever seen it. His face was covered in a growth of hair that was beyond stubble, but too patchy to be considered an actual beard. He was dressed in sweat pants and a baggy jumper. He looked pale, and there were dark circles around his eyes.

We exchanged a few perfunctory pleasantries before taking our drink outside to the beer garden on the riverside. There was no one else out there, which was a good thing as I knew that this was going to end in an argument.

'Why?' I asked as we sat looking out at the brown water of the river.

'You know then?' he said, taking another sip of his drink. 'I guessed you did when you called.'

'Why on Earth would you want to buy that place?' I said.

'My family needs a new house, here, and it was a great price.'

I shook my head.

'Because of all the fucking murders that have happened there, or did you forget about that?' I said, feeling the muscles in my face contracting in anger.

'No,' he said. 'I can't forget that house. I dream about it almost every night, and I couldn't take it anymore. I knew if I bought it, and lived there, I could prove to myself it's just a house.'

I thumped the table.

'That's just what it wants you to think,' I said. 'It draws us in, and makes us do terrible things, Wayne. For God's sake, think about your girls.'

He leant over and grabbed me by the collar.

'I am thinking about my girls,' he said, spitting in my face. 'Look at the state of me. Do you think having a father who looks and acts like this all the time is good for them? I can't sleep, I have no energy, I'm short-tempered all the time. Do you think that's a pleasant life for my daughters?'

He let me go, and I took a sip of my drink.

'It already has a hold on you,' I said. 'Can't you see it? You know what comes next.'

'It's just a fucking house,' he screamed at me. 'Bricks and mortar, nothing else. No ghoulies, no ghosties, and no fucking curses.'

'Then how do you explain everything that's happened?' I screamed back at him.

'Coincidence,' he said. 'Nothing more than that.'

'You really believe that?' I said.

'I have to,' he said. 'You know, you're the one who's obsessed with that place.'

He got up and left the table. He started to walk away, then stopped and looked back at me.

'Stay away from my family,' he said. 'And my house.'

With that, he was gone.

I went home and sat there trying to think of a way I could stop him, convince him that he was wrong, and that his life and those of his family were in danger. He was right, I was obsessed with that house, we all were, and had been since that night fifteen years earlier. Why could no one else see what was so clear to me?

Something dark had got inside us all, it started that night, and it was still there now, curled up inside us like a sleeping beast waiting to attack. It drew us back there to the house time after time. It had turned two of my closest friends into killers, and had turned Wayne into a stranger I could not even recognise.

It had to end, there had to be a way. Rob had tried destroying the old house, but it had not helped. Whatever it was, it was in the soil, the air, the land around the house. It could not be destroyed just by removing the house; it infected the new one as soon as it was built. I racked my brains to think of an answer. I had spent my whole life watching horror movies, and reading about the supernatural, surely somewhere tucked in a corner of my mind there had to be an answer.

Then it came to me. It was so obvious.

I waited until nighttime and then gathered the things I would need. I set off in the car, driving down that road was now second nature, I could have done it in my sleep. As I approached the house, I saw that there was a car in the driveway. Wayne was carrying a box from his car into the now uncovered door. All of the boards had gone; a few of the windows were lighted. I carried on driving towards the marsh, passing the house. I parked up further down the road and walked back, carrying the implements I needed to carry out my plan. Wayne's presence might delay me, but it was not going to stop me.

I stayed close to the hedgerows as I neared the house, hoping the night and my dark clothing would conceal me. Wayne came back out of the house and got another box from his car. When he returned to the house, I sneaked across the road and ran to the side of the house. This was closer than I had been to it since the old house was there. I felt that familiar queasiness that always seemed to come over me once I was in the garden. I cautiously moved along the wall. I looked through the window. I could see Wayne placing the boxes in the kitchen. None of the appliances were in place yet. I moved to the next window, this room was probably a dining room due to its proximity to the kitchen, though I could not tell for sure as the room was devoid of any furniture.

My spirits began to rise as I realised that Wayne and his family had not moved in yet. He was obviously just dropping a few things off in advance. All I had to do was wait for him to leave, and then I could go ahead with my plan. The queasiness was not going away, though, and I wanted to spend as little time in the garden as possible. I decided I would run back across the road and wait by the hedgerow a little way up, for Wayne to leave.

As I turned to run back to the road, I tripped over some sort of garden ornament and fell to the gravel floor with a thud. I was just about getting up when I heard a voice from behind me.

'Oi!' It was Wayne.

I tried to start running, but had twisted my ankle in the fall. I could hear Wayne's footfalls on the gravel behind me. He grabbed hold of the back of my hooded sweatshirt.

'What do you think you're doing?' he said as he spun me around. He saw it was me and looked confused. 'Chris?'

I had no choice. I swung around and hit him hard. He took a step backwards more surprised than hurt by my blow, but it made him let go of me. I bent down and grabbed a rock from the ground, and as he came at me again. I struck him with it on the side of the head. He went down instantly. I looked at him lying on the ground, a trickle of blood running from just above his ear, and for a moment I panicked. My decision to go to the house had been based on my desire to save Wayne and his family from himself, now he was on the floor bleeding. In my attempt to save him, had I just killed him?

I knelt down at his side and listened to his chest, not only could I hear his heartbeat I could also feel the rise and fall of his breathing. Thank God, he was alive. I took him under the arms and lifted slightly, then I dragged him across the drive, out of the gate and to the safety of the other side of the road. He would be all right there until I was done, and then he would thank me, I knew it.

I walked down and gathered up my things, the three full Jerry cans of petrol and the bag of flares. I walked back towards the house. This had to work, I had read about it so many times. When a place was so evil, so infected with darkness, the only way to get rid of it was purification by fire.

I used the first jerry can to soak as much of the downstairs of the house as I could, not wanting to linger inside too long. Even the brief time I was in there, I could hear the house screaming at me inside my mind. The queasiness increased dramatically inside the house. At one point, I had to stop to be sick. I coughed up some disgusting black substance, I hoped it was the darkness leaving me, being expelled from my body, just as I was about to expel it from this place.

I used the second two Jerry cans to soak the garden, letting the petrol absorb into the soil. Like I had said earlier, just getting rid of the house was not enough, the land had to be purified as well.

When I was done, I walked back across the road. Wayne was still where I had left him, he was starting to murmur now, it would not be long before he regained consciousness. I had to move quickly. I opened the bag of flares. I took the first one and struck it, its red light illuminating the area. I walked as close to the door as I dared and threw it inside. Instantly it made contact with the petrol and the hallway erupted in flames that soon spread to the other rooms. I walked to the side of the house and struck another flare, this one I launched into the garden at the back of the house. The fire spread like napalm over the grass. Finally, I walked back to the gate and threw the last flare into the front garden. The night was lit up by the inferno raging before me, and all at once, I felt a peace I had not experienced in years.

'No! God! No!' I heard from behind me. I turned to see Wayne rushing towards me. I thought that he would have felt the relief, too, that he would have seen that it was finally over. Instead, he looked hysterical in fear.

He tried to run past me, into the flaming driveway. I grabbed him and smiled at him.

'It's over, Wayne,' I said, ecstatic in my relief. 'It's finally over.'

'What have you done?' He screamed at me, his eyes full of fear and anger.

'I've got rid of the darkness.'

Wayne pushed me away and looked at the house.

'My girls are in there!' he screamed at me before running full pelt into the flames.

I stood there open mouthed. I looked at the upstairs window above the door. I saw them, two little silhouettes, black against the orange and raging flames. I dropped to my knees in defeat. The house had won, I was the one who had been pulled back to commit a great evil this time. I would never be free of the curse. Never.

FEAR AND LOATHING IN SKEG VEGAS

1

Most people turned to crime to fund their drug addiction. Paul Mayhew was not most people. He had turned to selling drugs to fund his gambling addiction. The drugs themselves he never touched, not even pot. No, for Paul, the drugs were just a means to an end. Once upon a time, he'd had a fairly good job. He'd been the assistant manager at the local Argos, until his gambling problem had become so bad that he was caught stealing from the tills to fund it.

It had started simply enough, when he was in college in Boston. In those days, he spent most of his time avoiding lectures in the student union bar, or 'The Horn Bar' as it was actually called. It was there that he had first started playing on the fruit machines. To begin with, it had just been a few quid here and there, but gradually it increased to everyday, and then all day everyday. The thrill of those little wins spurring him on, the promise of the big payout always just around the corner. The first time he'd won a jackpot, with a double repeater, had been the happiest day of his life up until that point hands down.

When he managed to get into university, he had found a small arcade around the corner from the campus. Not the garish kind he was used to back home in Skegness, with all the lights and computer games, no, this was one of those dark, dingy places with nothing but the gambling machines. He and his fellow addicts, of course at this point he hadn't realised he had a problem, spent hours on end feeding coins into those infernal machines. Once he had spent four hundred pounds of his eight hundred pound loan cheque in two hours. When at the end of this he had not won a thing, he had merely gone to the bank and drawn out the remainder of his cash.

At the end of his second year, he had dropped out and returned home to Skegness, where he managed to get the job at Argos. Skegness was a strange place, a costal town and holiday resort in the true British seaside tradition. It was not big enough to match up to the likes of Blackpool, but was still a popular destination for people from Nottingham and Yorkshire. Its popularity was something that had always confused Paul; to him it was just his hometown, as boring a place as anyone else's home.

In the summer it got to the point where you couldn't walk down the street sometimes for the sheer amount of bodies, all moving in and out of one tat shop after another. The nightlife in season could be bad as well, people were on holiday and relaxing, trouble often started.

By contrast, in the winter the place had an eerie and isolated quality. Sometimes it felt as if the place only really existed in the summer, and that during the winter the town and its residents were merely ghosts.

The problem for Paul was that there were so many arcades, with so many fruit machines, that there was no way to abate his need to gamble. Over the years, he had advanced to betting on the horses, he was a regular with every bookie in town, and to playing poker, online and in the pubs and clubs. Sometimes he would win fairly substantial amounts of money. In one poker tournament he had won nearly seven grand in a night. The only problem was that no sooner had he won the money than he was betting on something else, and more often than not losing it all.

This was the situation that had led him to start dealing on the side. He had made the acquaintance of one of the most successful, and brutal, of local dealers, a man simply known as Big Baz. The name was not ironic, Big Baz could easily have been called Fucking Enormous Baz, and it wouldn't be an understatement. He was a giant, at least six foot six and built like a brick shithouse. He was covered from head to foot in tattoos, not tasteful or arty ones, dirty homemade tattoos that you only seemed to find on the criminal classes. Baz had no front teeth and a nose that wouldn't have looked out of place on a boxer. He was always wearing tracksuits and baseball caps, and had two large Staffie dogs that he kept on large brass chains.

Paul was not ashamed to admit that the first time he had met the man mountain that was Big Baz , he had been terrified. Paul had been in one of the clubs on the sea front, that had long since closed down, enjoying a drink when he was approached by Baz.

'Oy you?' Baz had said towering over him. 'You work at Argos don't ya?'

Unable to speak due to his fear Paul had simply nodded.

'Yeah, thought so. Do you know that little scrote, Dennis?'

Again, Paul nodded.

'Have you seen him?' Baz asked.

Paul pointed over towards the bar area.

'Cheers,' Baz had said, wandering off to the bar with the kind of swagger that made him look even more ape like. Paul watched as he walked over to Dennis, who Paul agreed was a scrote. He worked at Argos during the summer, and was a pretentious twat of a sociology student who thought he could change the world.

Baz put one of his giant hands on Dennis's shoulder and dragged him back from the bar. Though there was no way on Earth that he could hear the conversation, it was clearly unpleasant. Baz was bending down to yell in the weedy little guy's face. He looked like a taut spring waiting to uncoil. Dennis, on the other hand, looked like a floundering fish, his hands gesticulating at speed as he tried to reason with the monster. Eventually, Baz tired of the conversation and smashed his beer bottle on the side of Dennis's head. Paul felt bad for leading Baz to him. Even if he was a bit of a dick, Dennis didn't deserve that.

One of the bouncers, one who'd been called in from out of town, had come over and tried to drag Baz out. Baz had head butted the guy in the face, flattening his nose. The other bouncers came dashing over and pulled their fallen comrade and Dennis away, undoubtedly to wait for ambulances. They left Baz well alone. They knew from personal experience that it was not worth confronting the dealer. He could do as he pleased, they even turned a blind eye to him dealing in the club, better that than ending up in hospital, or worse.

Baz grabbed another couple of beers from the bar, free of charge no doubt, and headed back towards Paul. He knew he was physically quaking with fear as the man approached. He knew he was next, guilty by association. What he had done to Dennis and the bouncer had not sated his blood lust.

Instead, he smiled and handed the second beer over to Paul.

'Cheers for pointing him out,' Baz said sitting down opposite him.

'No problem.'

'I've been looking for him for days. You would not believe how much money that little prick owes me.'

With that the two of them had got talking and, to some extent, become friends.

After he lost his job at Argos, Paul had approached Baz with a business proposition. Paul explained that through his university days he knew many of the middle class drug users around the area, those who would not want to associate with someone like Baz. If the drug dealer were to give him a commission, Paul would sell drugs on his behalf. Baz had loved the idea, and for the last few years that was how Paul had been paying his bills and feeding his habit. Now, though, he was in trouble, he had lost a poker tournament he had entered with Baz's money, and now he owed the dealer five grand, and had no way to pay.

2

Paul had spent the last few days in hiding, he hadn't dared to spend time in his little flat, instead he was staying at his mum's house. He wasn't sure if Baz knew where she lived, though knowing Baz's contacts he wouldn't have trouble finding that information out.

Paul's hope was that even a brute like Baz wouldn't want to smash a guy's skull in front of their mother.

His mother knew he was in trouble of some kind, she knew of his gambling problem, but didn't know he was selling drugs for the local psychopath. She was getting tired of him hanging around the house.

'Are you short of money again, love?' she asked.

'A little,' Paul replied.

She reached for her purse and drew out a twenty pound note.

'Will this help?' she said, handing the cash over to him.

'Yeah,' he lied. 'Thanks, Mum.'

'Go on get out of the house for a bit,' she said, it was more like a demand than a suggestion.

Paul slipped on his coat and headed out. He stuck to the side roads as he headed towards town. He didn't want to see Baz cruising through town in his BMW the way he liked to. He had no idea how he was going to get out of the situation he was in. He supposed he could take the twenty quid his mum had given him to the bookies and try to increase it to an amount he could enter another poker tournament with. He shook the idea away, it was that kind of thinking that had got him in this situation in the first place. No, his best plan was to talk to Baz, they had been friends for a few years now, Baz had always been reasonable with him. There was one problem with this—Baz was not reasonable with anyone who owed him money, let alone someone who owed him five grand. He would probably kill him, certainly put him in hospital.

As he approached town, Paul headed for The Lumley. It was the one place in town that he had never met Baz for a drink, he hoped that this meant that Baz was unlikely to turn up.

He walked into the bar and got himself a pint. There were several tables free. Paul chose the one in the corner, the most hidden from sight of the door, hoping if Baz came in and scanned the room he would not see him.

He finished his first pint and got another. He returned to the same table, from there he could see the fruit machine, its multicoloured lights blinking and flashing at him. Most people will look at these lights, they are sort of hypnotic, but to Paul watching them filled him with longing, a hunger that had to be satisfied.

For a while he tried to ignore it, the pulling sensation down in the pit of his stomach. He looked around the pub as his sipped his pint, watching the other people to distract himself from the fruit machine and its siren spell over him. There was an old man sat on his own, reading a paper and drinking bitter from a pint mug. There were a few younger lads playing pool and competing for the alpha male of the group status. There were a group of middle-aged men stood at the bar. They looked like they had money, business suits and expensive watches. There were a group of people, male and female, of various ages, all laughing and joking. From the way they behaved, Paul assumed that they were either a family group or coworkers. Finally, there was a young couple, chatting with each other, oblivious to everyone else. Paul tried to remember how long it had been since he had felt that close to someone, it must have been years. It was when he was still at university and had been going out with an art student called Harriet. God, he'd loved that girl. It had ended when he flunked out. She was unprepared to leave the city and go with him to Skegness, and he couldn't blame her.

The bitterness of the memory made him turn away from the young couple, and again he was staring at the fruit machine, its lights and noises calling to him like he was a sailor lost in the fog.

'Fuck it,' he said to himself as he stood up and pulled some change out of his pocket. He stood at the machine and dropped a few pound coins into the slot. He heard it drop straight to the bottom of the machine. To an experienced player like him, it was a beautiful sound, it meant that the prize fund was full and the money going in was bypassing it. It was ready to pay out.

He spun the wheels, feeling the surge of excitement that he always got when he thought he was on for a win. He was so engrossed in the game that he didn't notice the door open and Big Baz step in. He still had a pound credit in the machine when Baz grabbed him by the shoulder and dragged him backwards out of the pub.

Baz let him go once they were in the abandoned smoking area outside.

'You been avoiding me?' Baz asked. He seemed calm. This scared Paul more than if he'd seemed pissed off. When Baz was about to commit an act of brutal violence a strange kind of peace came over him.

'Course not, Baz,' Paul said. 'I've just been a bit sick lately.'

Baz nodded and lit a cigarette.

'Anything serious?' He asked.

'Just a bit of a cold, been staying at my mum's so she can look after me.'

'Did you sell that stuff yet?' Baz asked.

'Not all of it,' Paul lied. 'What with feeling shit and everything.'

'Well, I need whatever you've got left then,' Baz said.

'But I've promised it to one of my customers Baz, he's expecting it.'

'When?'

'When I'm well enough to take it to him,' Paul said.

'Well, I can get you some more in a few days, but I got a deal on tomorrow afternoon that means I need the stuff or the money to buy more,' Baz said. 'Which is it?'

'I can't get you either tonight, Baz,' Paul started to explain.

Baz grabbed him by the throat with one hand and swung him round so his back hit the wall of the pub.

'Are you trying to fuck me over?' Baz said, his eyes burning with sudden rage.

'No, Baz,' Paul choked.

'You better not be,' Baz said. 'I swear to God if you have pissed my money away down the bookies I will make sure you never fucking walk again.'

Paul was starting to feel light-headed, the pressure that Baz was exerting on his throat was stopping just enough air getting in to make him woozy.

'I want the money or the drugs tomorrow morning. Do you understand?' Baz said.

Paul nodded in response. He was no longer able to speak, if Baz didn't loosen his grip soon he was going to pass out.

'Bring one of them round my gaff by half nine,' Baz said. 'Or I'll tear this fucking shithole town apart to find you.'

Finally, Baz let go of his throat and Paul slid to the floor gasping for air. Baz leaned over him.

'Half nine at the latest,' he said.

Paul nodded and Baz walked away.

3

When he had dusted himself off a little and finally regained his breath, Paul headed back into the pub. As he approached the machine, he saw that one of those middle-aged businessmen was playing on the fruit machine. Not only that, but as the light flashed manically, Paul could tell that the man had just won the jackpot. Paul felt a flush of white-hot anger. He had left money in the machine; if Baz had not just dragged him out of the pub that jackpot would be his. He was not usually one for confrontation, but the incident outside had left him wound up. He stormed over to the businessman.

'Oi,' he said as he walked over. 'I still had money in there.'

The businessman looked him up and down, he regarded him with a look of pure disdain, like Paul was nothing but a bit of shit on his shoe.

'You left the pub,' the businessman said in a condescending tone. 'How was I supposed to know you were coming back?'

'I left the pub?' Paul said in disbelief. 'Did you see what happened? I was dragged out of the pub, against my will.'

'You still left,' the businessman said, smiling towards his friends at the bar.

'Well, you just robbed me of seventy quid,' Paul said. 'I still had money in the machine, that jackpot is mine.'

Paul was aware that people in the pub had stopped talking. The constant murmur of voices had ceased.

'Look, mate, I didn't even win it on your quid, I put two in after that,' the businessman said.

'So?' Paul said. 'I would have put more money in. You stole my game, and now you're stealing my money.'

The businessman rummaged in his suit pockets, he pulled out a pound coin and tossed it to Paul.

'There's your money back,' he said. 'Now fuck off.'

Paul stepped forward and grabbed the man's lapel.

'That's not enough, mate,' he said, his pulse racing and his jaw tense. 'Not nearly enough.'

'Out!' The barman said stepping from behind the bar. He put a hand on Paul's shoulder. 'Didn't you hear me? I said out.'

'Me?' Paul said in shock. 'He's the one who stole my money.'

'He gave you your quid back, take it and piss off,' the barman said. 'You're barred.'

Well, wasn't this a perfect little analogy for the state of this country? Paul thought to himself. He had done no wrong, in fact he'd been a victim of an assault, yet he was the one being punished. Meanwhile the man in the suit, who had robbed him blind, was not only getting away with it, he was being protected by those in a position of power. Conservative Britain at its best.

He could not be bothered to argue. He felt cheated and abused, but had no energy to fight his cause. Instead, he stormed out of the bar and into the cool winter air. The whole incident had soured his mood. He considered going home, but found him self ambling down chip pan alley. The aroma of chip fat and fish clung to the air down the road as it always did, even though most of the chip shops were closing for the evening. Paul carried on towards the clock tower near the sea front. He saw the embassy centre, the theater and pub complex, he considered going in the Litten Tree pub, but decided against it. He only had ten pounds left. That would get him two drinks at most. He saw the neon lights of all the arcades heading up to the pier. 'Why not?' he thought to himself. why not see if he could turn this ten pounds into something more? He crossed the road and entered the first arcade he came to. He walked past the endless rows of computer games and headed for the roped off area with all the signs saying that no one under eighteen was allowed to enter. This was where the big money gambling machines were kept. The ones with the seventy pound plus jackpots.

He was alone in the area and had the choice of machine. He went straight to his favourite, the deal or no deal machine, and started to pour in pound coins. The wheels went round and around. Several times he got onto the game board, but always went bust.

'We're closing in a couple of minutes,' a voice behind him said.

He turned around to see a young man in a fleece with the arcades logo on the chest.

Paul turned and waved at the young man, acknowledging the comment. He was down to his last few quid anyway. He hit the start button and carried on with his game.

As the arcade closed down Paul exited with nothing but his hands in his pockets. He knew now that he would have to get up early and leave town tomorrow, before Baz could find him. He would ask his mum to lend him some more money to get on a train, and he would get away for a while. He still had friends in Nottingham, from his university days, who would be willing to put him up for a while. Maybe he would try to get a job over there, but with his record that was unlikely.

4

He wandered the streets aimlessly, lost in his plans. Eventually he found himself stood on the end of the pier looking out to sea, and the distant, blinking lights of boats. Perhaps he should do that, get on a boat and go out to sea, find himself, get over this damned gambling habit, then he could start over.

'The problem with going out to sea to find yourself is you might not be the only thing you find,' said a voice at his side. He turned to see a man stood next to him. His age was difficult to discern as he wore a large, wiry beard and had a hood on. He looked disheveled, a tramp, Paul assumed.

'Excuse me?' Paul said, startled by the man's presence.

'You said you should go out to sea and find yourself,' the tramp said. His accent was English, but not recognisable to Paul. It sounded old fashioned. The words, though, troubled Paul, he could not remember saying them, he could only remember thinking it, but he guessed he must have been thinking out loud.

'It's a wonderous thing, the sea,' the tramp said. 'Spent many a year out there myself.'

Paul was not in the mood to listen to an old, vagrant mariner's tales. He wanted nothing more than some time to himself to finish planning how to get away from the serious beating that Baz was destined to give him tomorrow.

'Well, I have to be going,' he said, but the tramp put his hand on his arm. Even through his coat, the hand felt cold and damp. A shiver, like a little electric shock, ran up his arm. For some reason he could not understand, Paul felt scared all of a sudden. More scared than he had ever felt before.

'There are many wonderous things out there,' the tramp repeated. 'And, many things that would turn your soul icy and cold. Things most people never see, things most people don't even know exist.'

Paul tried to pull his arm free, but the tramp tightened his grip.

'I've seen them, though, I've seen the lot of them, Paul,' the tramp continued. Paul barely registered that the tramp was using his name, he was just so terrified.

'Once you've seen them, you can't ever forget them. They change you, Paul, change your very essence. It's so long since I've been home, I doubt it's even there anymore. Now all I do is travel around and do their bidding. A slave to the sea. A slave to the cold. A slave to them.'

Paul was freezing. It was like his arm was turning to ice where the tramp had hold of him. The cold was spreading through his veins. It was getting hard to breathe. Paul was sure that if he were to look in a mirror he would be turning blue.

'Once the sea has you, Paul, it won't let you go. It drains your blood and fills your veins with ice-cold brine. It takes your humanity, your very soul and makes you something else. I never wanted to be this Paul, I never wanted to be the harbinger of doom for those fucking monsters, but here I am.'

Paul could hear his own heartbeat in his ears, despite his terror it was slowing down. He was certain he was getting hyperthermia.

'There is one thing they allow me to do, though, Paul, they allow me the chance to save one soul, a single survivor. I've chosen you, Paul, you can escape what's coming.'

The tramp let go of his arm and Paul staggered backwards. He fell back against the railing and only just managed to stay upright. He couldn't feel his arm. It was like it was frozen solid. He gasped for breath, trying to fill his lungs. It had felt almost like he was drowning. The tramp approached. He reached into his pocket and pulled out a large gold coin. To Paul, it looked like something from a pirate film.

'Here's your chance, Paul,' the tramp said smiling, showing his blackened teeth. 'I know you're a gambling man, so you'll take the chance. You only get one, though, that's it and then I'm gone. So what'll it be, Paul, heads or tails?'

Paul didn't know what was happening, his body was still reeling from that frozen grip the tramp had put on him. He was just starting to get a pins and needles feeling in his arm as it came back to life.

'Heads,' he said.

The tramp nodded and flicked the coin high into the air. It went spinning upwards, disappearing into the darkness of the night. It was a moment that seemed to last forever, time slowing down, the night was strangely silent.

Then the coin came crashing to the ground. The sound was deafening, like a hammer hitting an anvil. Paul covered his ears to protect them from the sound. The tramp stepped over and looked down at the coin.

'You're a lucky man, Paul,' he said. 'Now get out of here.'

Paul didn't need telling twice. He set off running, not even thinking where he was going. The tramp began to laugh, the sound carried with Paul until he reached the sand of the beach, then abruptly stopped. Paul was panting from the run. He turned and looked back at the pier. The tramp was nowhere to be seen, despite the fact that the spot they had been stood in was well illuminated.

Paul shook his head, he found it hard to believe that the whole thing had actually happened. Perhaps it had been some kind of hallucination. Perhaps he was losing his mind. It would not surprise him, with all the stress he was under anyone would snap. The problem with this explanation was that his arm still felt cold, nowhere near as cold as it had been, yet still cooler than the rest of his body.

He tried to remember the things that the tramp had said, but they had seemed like delusional ravings, Paul had been too scared to truly let the words sink into his mind. He remembered that he had won a coin toss, and that meant he was saved, but he had no idea from what.

He walked down the beach, towards the sea. It was low tide, and as everyone who has ever been to Skegness knows, that means a long walk to the sea. He stood there in the cold sea breeze, smelling the salty air, hoping it would clear his head. He had real problems. How was he going to get away from Baz? He did not have the time to be worrying about the crazy talk of some mad tramp. He needed a plan and he needed one quick, he looked at his watch and saw that it was nearly midnight, he only had about nine hours to get away, before Baz came looking for him.

He stood at the line of the sea. It gently lapped at his shoes as the tide began to turn. He looked down at the gentle foam, and saw something. Every so often in the water he saw small flickers of blue light, about the size of a pin prick. The first few times he thought it was his imagination, or a trick of his eyes. Then he saw them again, and again, and again, thousands of them blinking bright blue in the dark water. He looked up and down the line of the beach. They were everywhere.

He bent over and stuck his hand into the water, which was cold but not as cold as the tramp's grip had been. He swilled his hand around in the water, seeing the blue flashes brighter as he did this. When he pulled his hand out of the sea, it was covered in a gelatinous clear substance. It felt strange. It clung to his hand, and yet was not sticky to the touch. He saw the flashes within the substance, dim at first, but when he touched it they grew brighter. He rubbed his hand on his trousers, wiping the mysterious goo off his skin.

He had no idea what these things were, he guessed that maybe it was some kind of jellyfish spawn, but then he did not ever remember hearing of such a thing. All of a sudden he felt very vulnerable out there on the beach alone at night. It was something he had done a million times, and it had never bothered him before. The worst you were likely to encounter was Mad Mike, who lived in a tent on the beach with his equally mad mother. Mike was harmless, though, he just talked to himself. Tonight, though, after all that had occurred with Baz and the tramp and now this strange illuminating slime, he felt that he needed to be away from here. He headed home.

5

His sleep that night was restless, and filled with awful dreams. He dreamt of Baz chasing him down the street with an axe. Crowds of people just stood and watched, almost complicit in their inaction.

Then he dreamt of his mother, they were on a boat together in the dream, and she fell overboard. As much as Paul fought to save her, something was fighting against him, dragging her down into the depths.

Then he dreamt of a cold dark place under the sea, ruled by unspeakable beings, cruel beings. He knew he shouldn't be there. If they were to find him, he would be turned just like the tramp, yet he could not find his way home.

He woke to the sound of his alarm bleeping. He leant over and switched it off. It was seven in the morning, he had two hours to get some money off his mother, pack, and get the hell out of Skegness before Baz caught up with him, demanding either the money, the drugs or Paul's blood.

He quickly got up, washed and dressed. He walked to the kitchen, expecting his mother to be reading the paper and drinking coffee. His mother had always been a creature of habit. She was always up at six-thirty and then she would read the papers and drink coffee. It was a ritual he had never known to be broken in his whole life. It was as certain as the seasons, or the tide of the sea.

Thinking of the sea scared him. Images from his nightmares flooded his mind. He worried for his mother's safety. It was because of the dream of the boat trip. He brushed the feeling aside, assuming that there must be a logical explanation for his mother's absence. He walked to her bedroom and gently knocked on the door.

'Mum?' he said. 'Mum, are you okay?'

He waited, but no reply came.

He tried knocking once more, a little louder, but still there was silence from the other side of the door. Gently he pushed the door open, expecting to see the room dark and his mother asleep. The room, however, was light, and the bed was made. She had got up as normal, then where was she?

The papers, he thought, perhaps they hadn't been delivered and she had gone down to the newsagents to get them. This was plausible, his mother was so set in her ways that if the papers weren't there she would have to go and fetch them before she could get on with her day.

He looked at his watch. It was quarter past seven. How long would she be? He really didn't have the time to wait for her, not today, he decided it was best that he headed to the newsagents with the hope of catching her on her way home. He took the bag he had packed with him, so he could be on the first train out of town.

The first thing that struck him when he got outside was the stillness of the air. Skegness had a slogan, 'It's so bracing,' this was because it was always windy there. Even in the height of summer, there was a breeze that crept in from the sea. That was why they'd built that wind farm just off the coast a few years back. Today, though, the air didn't move at all.

The second thing was the sound, or more importantly the lack of it. The road that mum lived on was usually quiet, but you could still hear the traffic from the main road, which was quite close by. Today, though, he could hear nothing. Something felt wrong.

Paul tried to ignore this feeling, shaking it off as the remnants of his bad dreams, the way that sometimes nightmares can linger with you for the rest of the day. He set off towards the newsagents, hat pulled down low and hood up, just in case Baz was already about.

When he got to the road the newsagents was on, he was surprised to see that there was no traffic. There were cars parked on the side of the road, but none traveling. This really was strange, by this time the road was usually full of 4X4's driven by middle class women taking their children to the primary school round the corner. Paul knew because he always felt sorry for those kids. When he was young his mum would drop him off at school just before nine, nowadays, though, it seemed like all schools opened early and children would often be there two hours before lessons started.

Today there were no 4X4's, no middle class mothers, no children, nobody at all. The pavements were as deserted as the roads. Paul was starting to feel very ill at ease. Where was everyone? Sure, it was early by his normal standards, but not for most of the working population. He continued walking down the silent street to the newsagents. When he went inside, he found it, too, was completely devoid of life. The door was unlocked but there was no one in there, no customers, not even a shop assistant.

Paul was felt a trickle of cold sweat run down his neck, followed by a shudder. He knew he had to keep it together, but he could feel panic chomping at the bit to take control of him. He left the newsagents and returned to the empty street. He stood there trying to decide what to do. It was so still, so silent. Then he heard it, faintly at first, but definitely there, a faint hum in the distance, like some kind of electronic drone. It was almost at a frequency to low for human hearing to register, but it was just audible.

He tried to determine the direction the sound was originating from. After a little while, he realised it was coming from the East, from the sea. He had not wanted to go near the sea, not after all the strange things that had happened last night, and not with Baz out for his blood. He wanted to get on a train and get away. Priorities have to change some times, though. Not only was the town seemingly deserted, one of the missing was his own mother, he had to find her.

He set off towards the town, not quite jogging, but walking very quickly. When he reached the train station and the convergence of main roads by it, he was amazed to see that the road was as devoid of traffic as the others. He had hoped that it had just been a quiet day, that there was a logical explanation for what was happening, but now seeing the main road into town without a single moving car on it, he knew that it was real. Or was it? For a brief moment, he hoped that all of this was just another nightmare, and that soon his alarm would wake him for real. He would walk into the kitchen and his mother would be sat reading the paper with a coffee cup in her hand. She would offer to make him breakfast and he could continue with his plan.

Deep down, though, he knew this wasn't a dream. Everything was recognisable and things were happening in real time, not the disjointed manner they occur in dreams. He continued walking, past K.F.C and down into chip pan alley again. When he got to the Hildred's shopping centre at the end of the road, he could hear the hum more clearly. Not only that, he could see the light emanating from the beach. It was faint, as it was day light, but the dull grey sky seemed to be lighting up with a bright blue, rhythmic pulse. The colour made him remember the strange lights he had seen flickering in the surf the previous night. The lights in the gel he had on his hand.

He felt his heart pumping in his chest. He did not want to go any further, but he had to. He had to find his mother. He took a deep breath and tried to harness his fear, turn it into motivation. He set off running for the sea front.

6

The sight that greeted him as he arrived on the beach was like nothing he had ever seen. There, in one large group, stood the entire population of the seaside town of Skegness. He recognised friends, old teachers, ex-girlfiends, customers, and even Baz. None of them was moving, none of them was speaking, they all merely stood there, facing the same way, staring out to sea. Paul tried waving his hand in front of the faces of a few of his friends, they did not even flinch, it was like they were frozen in time. He ran through the crowd, which must have totaled ten thousand people, desperate to find his mother. It was like looking for a needle in a stack of needles. He would spot a figure of a similar build, with similar hair and go racing over to them, only to find they were a stranger.

He ran to the front of the crowd, it ended just at the sea. He looked out, the sea was glowing blue in regular pulses. It was coming from below the water, and he got the sense that it was getting closer. He turned back to the crowd, and against all the odds, he saw her. She was about five hundred meters back, and two hundred to his right. He raced over to her. He took her face in his hands and kissed her.

'Mum?' He said clicking his fingers in her face. 'Can you hear me?'

Her face showed not even a glint of recognition. Her gaze was fixed on the sea, on the light, on whatever was coming.

'Sorry for this, mum,' he said, and then he slapped her hard across the face, so hard that her head turned. She merely turned it back and continued to look at the sea.

'Fuck!' He screamed.

Well, if he couldn't get her to walk off the beach he would carry her. He bent down to pick her up in a fireman's lift, yet when he lifted nothing happened. His mother was a petite woman, she always had been. He should have been able to lift her easily, but no matter how hard he strained he could not mover her, it was as if she was welded to the floor. Stood nearby was a child, no older than five. He tried to lift the child; he, too, would not budge.

'You can't save them, Paul,' a familiar voice said behind him. He turned and saw the tramp. 'I told you I can only save one.'

'You did this!' Paul said, his fear becoming rage. He charged at the tramp. The bearded man simply put his hand out and stopped Paul dead. The cold, dampness of his touch felt a thousand times worse on his chest.

'Let's get something straight,' the tramp said angrily. 'I did not do this. I merely pave the way. If it wasn't me, it would be someone else. They will come no matter what, they always have. At least I get the chance to save one soul. I wish I could do more but I can't.'

'Why me?' Paul screamed.

'Because you were there,' the tramp said. 'Right time, right place. Chance, pure luck.'

'What's happening?' Paul said, tears starting to flow.

'They're coming. They're coming to feed. Like always, they will suck the life force and souls out of every man, woman and child. Everyone, except you.

Paul looked at the sea, the light was even brighter now. Looking at it was starting to hurt his eyes.

All around him, the crowd began to move en masse towards the sea. They all kept the same pace, like a giant army marching into the sea.

'It's time,' the tramp said. 'Praise be to my master, and God help these poor souls.'

Paul watched in horror as the people walked into the water until it was above their heads. Onwards the crowd pushed, his mother now was walking into the water. He watched as it rose up her body with each step, until the last grey curl on her head was submerged. The tears flowed endlessly from his red eyes. The tramp kept the freezing hand on his chest.

The whole process took about twenty minutes, then they were all gone, the only two beings left on the beach were Paul and the tramp. The bearded man lowered his hand from Paul's chest and he dropped to his knees. The tramp stood over him.

'I'm sorry for your loss,' the tramp said. 'I have to go, too, now.'

Paul watched as the tramp walked into the water. Just before his head was submerged, he turned and offered Paul a look of pity. Then he was gone.

On the still and silent beach, in the still and silent town, a single lonely figure knelt on the sand and sobbed.

TRACKS

'Here it is,' Steve signed as they stopped their bikes as the bottom of the bridge. 'Come on.'

Jake got off his bike and they dumped them on the grass verge at the side of the road. Steve turned to his younger brother and moved his hands.

'Come on, let's go up,' he signed.

Jake followed his big brother up the slope of the railway bridge. Jake had been born deaf, he never knew any different. His parents and Steve could all hear, but they had all learnt B.S.L. in order to communicate with Jake. Jake was only twelve, whereas Steve was sixteen. Jake looked up to him in the way only a little brother can. Steve was his hero, his model for how to be. Whatever Steve was interested in, Jake followed suit.

When they reached the top of the bridge, Jake looked around. The road continued over it, and there was only a narrow path for them to stand on. If two cars tried to come over at the same time, at least one of them would have to mount the path, as this was a single lane country road. Jake knew, though, that if Steve heard a car coming he would make sure that Jake was all right, he always looked out for him.

'Has anyone ever told you the story of Alison Rawlins?' Steve signed at his brother.

'No,' Jake signed back. 'Who is she?'

'She was the most beautiful girl in the whole village,' Steve signed. 'I was only about eight when she died, so you'd have only been four, but I remember seeing her. She had this amazing long blonde hair that flowed down her back. When the sunlight hit it, it was blinding.'

'What happened to her?' Jake asked.

'For some reason she was really sad. Some people say that she was mentally ill. Others say that a boy from town broke her heart and she just couldn't carry on. She came down to this bridge late one night, and walked down the bank over there.' Steve pointed to the slope that led off the edge of the bridge. It was covered with bushes and trees, but Jake could see there was a thin path that led all the way down. He looked back to Steve.

'She went onto the tracks,' Steve continued. 'She walked right into the middle of the tunnel and waited. A little while later a train came along, there was no way the driver could see her in time, what with her being stood in the tunnel. He saw her at the last second and slam, the train hit her. They say that it nearly tore her to pieces.'

Jake gulped, the idea of being ripped apart by a high speed train was terrifying. Poor Alison must have been in agony.

'Some of the older kids, the ones who knew her, started coming down here and looking down in the tunnel,' Steve continued. 'I don't know whether it was because they missed her, or just out of morbid curiosity. They said that if you walked right into the middle of the tunnel and stood on the tracks, the exact spot where the train hit Alison, closed your eyes and counted to ten. When you opened your eyes, you would see Alison's ghost, all bloody and disgusting. They said she would reach out for you, and if she caught you, she'd kill you. I guess she was lonely in death.'

Jake looked over the side of the bridge down at the tracks and shivered. He knew that he was too old to be scared of ghost stories, but something about this story had really creeped him out. He turned back to Steve.

'Have you ever done it?' Jake asked.

Steve nodded.

'I tried once,' Steve signed. 'It was when I was your age, I stood there in the tunnel with my eyes closed, and I started counting. I could hear someone walking up behind me as I counted. I got so scared that I ran out of there with my eyes still closed and didn't open them until I was back on the bank.'

Jake was shocked. He had always seen Steve as so brave, and yet he had chickened out. It must have been really scary down there.

'Anyway,' Steve signed. 'We better get home. Mum'll have lunch on by now.'

They walked back down to their bikes and then rode the half mile back to the village and down their road.

When they got home, Mum had indeed nearly finished cooking Sunday lunch. Their Dad was out in his workshop making a chair. He was not a professional carpenter, but had been doing it as a hobby for about five years now. The furniture he made was actually quite good; he sold it online in an eBay shop.

Mum turned round to them as they stepped through the kitchen door. She signed and spoke at the same time, as they all tended to do.

'Where have you been?'

'Just riding our bikes,' Steve replied.

'Well you better both go and have a wash, dinner will be ready soon,' she said and signed. She turned to Jake. 'Would you go and let your Dad know dinner is nearly ready when you're done, Jake?'

Jake nodded, and then both boys ran up the stairs. There were two bathrooms upstairs, one on the landing and one in their parents' room, so they didn't need to fight over who went first. Steve ran to their parents' room and Jake went to the bathroom on the landing. He shut the door behind him and filled up the sink. As he washed his face and hands, he thought about the bridge, and the story of Alison Rawlins, and her ghost. He shuddered once more at the thought of being hit by a train. He had watched them going past plenty of times, the size of them and the speed. No wonder they said it had made a mess of the poor girl.

He wondered why she had chosen to do it. He knew that sometimes people got so sad that they ended their own live. He didn't understand it. How could anyone feel that bad, sometimes he felt sad about the fact that he couldn't hear, especially when his family spoke about music. He wished he could hear music. He felt some vibrations from it, but it wasn't the same. Even when he had felt at his worst, though, the thought of killing himself had never entered his mind. These people must have had some awful problems to feel that it was their only option.

The other thing that Jake couldn't understand about Alison Rawlins was even if she felt that low that killing her self was her only option, why one Earth would she choose to do it in such a horrendous way. Jake thought that people just took tablets and went to sleep.

He looked in the mirror and imagined what it was like down in the tunnel, stood there with your eyes closed counting to ten as Alison's ghost approached you. He imagined her twisted, ruined body shuffling towards him.

He opened his eyes and shook the image away. He couldn't believe that Steve had run out of the tunnel before getting to ten. Jake had always thought of his brother as brave. Knowing this fact made him feel a little disappointed, like a part of the way he saw the world had gone away.

Could he do it? Would he be able to do what his brother had not? He knew he would be scared, but he had to admit that he thought that maybe he could. He had an advantage you see. Steve had said that he had got too scared because he could hear something shuffling up the tracks towards him. That was why he had run out of the tunnel. Jake, though, wouldn't have that problem. He was deaf, and would not hear the sounds.

He put the idea to the back of his mind and dried his hands and face. Steve was in his bedroom when Jake stepped back out on to the landing. Jake went down the stairs and then walked out of the front door. He walked around to the side of the house, where his Dad's workshop sat. Once upon a time, it had been the garage, but Dad had extended it and turned it into somewhere to make his furniture.

As he opened the door, he saw that his Dad had his back to him and was using one of the machines, the big saw. Jake did what he always did, he flicked the light on and off quickly. This was the code the system they had come up with for Jake to get his dad's attention when he was working. It would be too dangerous for Jake to just tap him on the back, and

Jake didn't like shouting. He had no idea what sound he was making, and this always bothered him.

His Dad turned around when he noticed the flashing light. He smiled at Jake.

'Hey, Jake,' he signed. 'I take it dinner's nearly ready?'

'Yeah, Mum told me to come get you,' Jake replied.

'Ok,' Dad said then switched off the saw. 'What you been doing today?'

'Me and Steve went and road our bikes.'

'Where did you go?' Dad asked.

'All over,' Jake said. 'Have you heard of Alison Rawlins?'

Dad looked concerned.

'Did you go out to the bridge?' He asked.

Jake nodded. He was always unable to lie to his Dad.

'I know that the kids have come up with some stupid ghost story about that bridge. What happened to poor Alison was terrible, but there's no such thing as ghosts.'

Jake wasn't so sure. If ghosts didn't exist, why were there so many stories about them?

'I want you to promise me you'll never go into that tunnel,' Dad said. 'It would be dangerous for anyone, but especially you. If a train was coming, you wouldn't be able to hear it.'

His imagined picture of the mangled ghost of Alison Rawlins sprang into his mind again. He pushed the thought away. He knew his dad was right, but still, he wanted to prove to himself that he could do something that Steve had failed to do.

'I promise,' he signed to his Dad, even though he thought it was a promise he might have to break.

'Good boy,' Dad said.

They ate dinner as a family, and as always it was the one time that Jake felt the most left out. They would often carry on talking amongst themselves while they ate. The fact that they were holding and using cutlery meant they were unable to sign. Jake had started learning to lip read, but this was made more difficult when people had mouths full of food. So he often ended up sitting there eating his dinner with no idea what they were talking about. On his more paranoid days, he would imagine that they were talking about him, but he doubted that was really the case. Periodically one of them would remember that he existed and sign something to him, he would then reply. Then they would all carry on eating and talking amongst themselves.

After dinner, Steve washed up and he dried and put away, while Mum took what she referred to as her 'well-earned rest.' Dad went back out to the workshop to continue with whatever he was making.

'Shall we go and play football in a bit?' Jake asked Steve.

His older brother shook his head.

'Sorry, Jake,' he signed. 'I'm going round a friend from schools house. We'll play tomorrow, though.'

Jake often wished that he could go to Steve's friends' houses with him, but knew that it was not cool to drag your little brother around with you all the time. Steve was so good to him, playing with him far more than he probably wanted to at his age, that he did not begrudge him some time to himself.

When they had finished the washing up, Steve left for his friend's house. Jake went out into the back garden and kicked the ball around on his own for a while, but it wasn't the same.

His mind kept drifting back to the bridge, and the tunnel and the ghost of Alison Rawlins. He thought that maybe if he went and proved he could face her ghost, that Steve would be so impressed that maybe he would take him out with his friends sometimes.

Jake ran into the house and told his mum that he was going for another bike ride. She looked at him and frowned. She never liked it when he went out without Steve. She worried about him not hearing cars that were near him.

'I'm not sure that's a good idea,' she signed.

'But Mum,' Jake replied, 'I have mirrors all over my bike and I'm always really careful. Please can I go?'

Mum sighed.

'Alright, but don't go to far and be back before it gets dark,' she said.

Jake hugged her and then ran off outside and grabbed his bike.

When he reached the bridge, he left his bike in the same spot that he had done earlier. The bright sunlight that had been there when he left the house had dulled off a little as the sky had clouded over. A slight breeze blew in his face as he approached the path down the bank.

All of a sudden, as he looked down the narrow path that snaked down to the railway tracks, Jake felt less sure of his own bravery. Even the trip down the path now looked scary. The trees and bushes that surrounded it were the perfect place for someone, or something, to be hiding in wait for him. He pictured himself walking down the path, and an arm of rotting flesh reaching out and dragging him into one of the bushes. He would never be seen again. He would become a local legend himself, the little deaf boy who disappeared one Sunday afternoon.

He told himself he was being stupid. The ghost of Alison Rawlins was supposed to haunt the tunnel, not this path, so why would a dead arm grab him from the bushes? He forced himself to begin the descent to the tracks.

When he got to the bottom of the path, he looked up the tracks. They were straight and he could see for miles this direction. There was no sign of any trains, so he walked onto the tracks and headed towards the tunnel.

The arch of its opening looked like a wide, hungry mouth ready to devour him. The tunnel was not that long, only about forty feet, so he could clearly see the sunlight and the track on the other side. There was no sign of a train in this direction either. He looked behind himself just to check and saw that it was fine. He took a deep breath to steady his nerves and stepped into the tunnel.

Instantly as he stepped inside he felt how much cooler the air was in here. The wind seemed to swirl around inside the tunnel, making it feel even more chilly. He looked at the walls of tunnel. On the left hand side someone had spray painted 'Alison will get you' in red on the wall. He shuddered. Perhaps this was a bad idea. Perhaps he would be better off going home right now. No one knew he was here, so no one need ever know that he had chickened out.

He would know, though, and he would hate himself for it. This was the first chance he had in his life to do something his older brother had not been able to do. He loved Steve, but like everyone, there was sibling rivalry, and this was an important moment for Jake.

He carried on along the tracks hoping he would be able to tell the exact spot he had to stand. He needn't worry, whoever had spray painted the warning on the wall had also marked the exact spot he need to be on.

Jake positioned himself on the red mark they had sprayed onto the track. He took one last look up the track, in both directions, and saw that it was clear. He closed his eyes and began to count in his mind.

One.

Two.

Three.

He felt something, he couldn't explain it. It was just a sense that he was not alone, a vibration in the air. He felt his heart pounding in his chest as he imagined her shuffling up the tracks towards him.

Four.

Five.

Six.

There was a smell now, something he could not quite place, but that had not been there a moment ago. It smelt like decay.

Seven.

Eight.

Nine.

The hairs on the back of his neck stood up as he felt her hot breath on his flesh. A voice in his head screamed at him to run, there was no shame in running. People are meant to run away from things like this. He told the voice to shut up. He was terrified, but he had to do this. He had to finish.

Ten.

Jake opened his eyes. There was nothing in front of him. He had feared that as soon as his eyes were open she would be there.

He sighed a little, but then felt the hot breath on the back of his neck again. He turned around slowly.

The things he had imagined, the horrors his mind had created when he thought about what she would look like, were nothing in comparison to what he saw.

There she stood, her body twisted at the waist, several of her ribs protruded through her grey oily skin. One arm was missing; there was just a spaghetti like mass of torn skin and sinew hanging from the stump. Her neck had been broken and her head hung at a funny angle. Her lower jaw had been detached, and hung, flapping by a small amount of skin on one side. Her black, massive tongue lolled around free of the prison of the jaw. One eye was grey and milky in its socket, the other hung from the optic nerve halfway down her face. Yellow crud oozed from the gaping socket. The top of her skull was flapping open revealing her brain. The beautiful, blonde hair that Steve had described was now dirty and matted with dried blood.

Jake tried to breathe, but could not take in any air. It was as if she was swallowing up all of the life around him. He felt his bladder release and the warmth of his urine wetting the front of his trousers.

Her one gnarled arm lifted up and reached out for him, her bony fingers trying to grab hold of him.

The voice in his head was telling him he had to run. 'If she catches you, she kills you.' This was what Steve had said earlier, Steve who had not been brave enough to finish counting. Steve who had been spared this horror. Steve who right now was probably playing computer games with his friends whilst his little brother was in a railway tunnel about to be murdered by this foul entity.

He wanted to run, but he could not move, so great was his fear. She leaned closer, the smell of death surrounding him. Her outstretched finger caught hold of the collar of his shirt, and with great ease she lifted him up. She pulled him closer to her. Jake knew that this was it, this was the end.

Suddenly she swung him hard to the side and let go her grip. Jake flew through the air like a discarded doll. He felt a thud and his back collided with the wall of the tunnel. He slid down the wall and collapsed on the gravel at the side of the tracks.

Alison Rawlins looked at him, and then she was engulfed in blue. The air was sucked away from Jake and vibrations shook him violently. The chill of the tunnel was replaced with heat, and the smell of death was replaced with the hot smell of engines.

The train sped past him, unaware of his presence. He watched it go by, amazed that he was still alive. If she hadn't have tossed him aside the train would have hit him for sure.

When the train left the tunnel, there was no trace of Alison. She had vanished as quickly as she appeared. Jake got to his feet and ran out of the tunnel. He climbed the bank as quickly as he could and grabbed his bike.

He pedaled as fast as his shaken legs could manage. He had braved the tunnel. He had counted to ten and he had seen the ghost of Alison Rawlins. He knew the truth now. She was not some murderous spirit. She was a protector, stopping people from dying in the same horrendous way she had. Alison Rawlins had saved Jake's life, and that was something he would never forget.

THE CROWS

They're mocking me. The crows. I can hear it in their malicious cawing; it's as though they are laughing right at my face. I look around me, flat expanses of field for miles, glowing in the uncharacteristically hot spring sun. A trickle of sweat runs down my aching face. One of the crows caws loudly off to my right, and soon they all join in, a cacophony of sound that makes my head hurt, and my mind itch. At first there had only been a few, and they had been wary, but soon they had grown in confidence, gorging themselves on the freshly sown seeds, then their friends had turned up. A message had gone out on the great crow grapevine that there was a delectable feast to be had in Harper's field, and all I could do was watch.

God I was thirsty. I seemed so long since I'd last had a drink, and the sun was beating down at full strength. I guess I have no one to blame but myself for my situation, well no one except that bastard Harper. It should have been so straight forward, a simple job that would keep me financially secure for years, but there's no such thing as simple job.

I'd first heard about Harper's gold in the local pub. A group of the locals had been talking about weird old Harper. I had only lived in the village a year, but knew well enough that the hulking great farmer had a reputation for being odd. Firstly, he lived all on his own in that big farm house just outside the village, he had lived there all his life. After his parents died, he had inherited the house and the farm. The other odd thing was that not one single person had ever heard him speak, not even the shop owner. Once a week Harper came into the shop and bought his groceries, but never once had he even said so much as thank you to the shop owner.

To me, a city boy, all of the locals had seemed odd, but Harper was definitely the strangest. The first time I had encountered him I had been crossing the road to get to the post office. Harper had been coming down the road in his beaten up, old Land Rover. I swear to God, that when he saw me in the road, he smiled and sped up. I had to run and jump out of his way to avoid being hit by him. I took exception to this and shouted after him.

'Watch it, wanker!' I had yelled.

Then the brake lights had come on. The Land Rover began to creep backwards, slowly, heading for where I stood at the side of the road with my heart still racing. When he pulled up along side me, I could see just how big he was. He looked like one of those guys you see on the World's Strongest Man competition at Christmas, only he was disheveled in his dirty brown corduroy trousers, tatty green sweater, torn wax jacket and filthy tweed flat cap. His thick curly hair was black, but speckled with a frosting of grey. He looked filthy, as though it had been years since he had even seen a bath, let alone had one. He looked me in the eyes, his face betraying no emotion. There was something about the way he looked at me, that made me look to my feet. I heard him laugh and then drive off.

A few weeks later, I had been discussing the incident with a few of the regulars in the local pub.

They had joked that I was lucky to be alive. Harper was crazy, they said. His mother had grown up in the village, but his father was an outsider. They said that when Mr Harper senior had first moved to the village, he had the the hint of a foreign accent, they couldn't quite agree on what sort. Some felt it was German, others said Russian, one even suggested it was Swedish. The only thing they agreed on was that Harper wasn't his real name, they believed he'd assumed it to sound more English, apparently within months of moving to the village, his accent was gone. He married a young woman from the village and bought out her family's farm. They had one child, the monstrosity that had tried to kill me with his Land Rover, and kept themselves to themselves.

However, they had not been so isolated as their son was to become. They would, on occasion, come to the pub or ask for assistance from on of the local tradesmen. It was one of these, Mickey Welby, a plumber, who had been the first to suggest the secret of the gold. He had gone up to the farm house to fix a water leak, old man Harper had to pay him with money out of the safe. Mickey had sneaked a look as the safe door opened and saw a stack of gold.

'It was those bars you see in all the films,' Mickey, now seventy-five, had told me.

'Ingots' I said.

'No, it's the truth,' he said defensively.

'No, the gold bars are called ingots,' I explained.

'Oh right, yes then it was ingots,' Mickey said smiling. 'I remember it clear as day, there was stacks of the stuff, at least sixty bars.'

I wanted to put the rumours down to nothing more than Mickey's overactive imagination, and village gossip, but I couldn't. The tale of a ton of gold in a safe was like a red flag to a bull for me. I'd moved here to go straight, get away from that life. Six big bank jobs and I'd never been arrested. It was only a matter of time, though. I decided to get out while the going was good, leave London, come to Lincolnshire. Buying the house had eaten up most of the money I'd made, though, and if things carried on getting more expensive I'd soon have to go out and get a proper job.

At first that idea had appealed to me, it was something I'd never done, and I would be able to prove to myself I really was going straight. Harper's gold kept going through my mind, though. It would be so easy, it was sure to be an old safe, the sort I could crack with my eyes closed, and if there was only a quarter as much gold as Mickey suggested, at the price it was at the moment, I'd be set for life. There was no real decision to make.

I started watching Harper's farm, trying to figure out the best ways in and out. I timed how long the fucking ogre spent doing his weekly shop. It took him an hour and a half to drive to the village, do his shopping, pack it into his car and get back to his front door. It wasn't long, but I thought it would be long enough.

The week before I planned to do the job I waited for him to pull out of his driveway and then scouted out the house. There were no alarm boxes or wires, and when I knocked on the door there wasn't a sound, he obviously had no dogs. Out of curiosity, I tried the door. To my astonishment it opened. I laughed to myself; the idiot didn't even bother locking his doors. This really would be like taking sweets from a baby. I took the opportunity to go in and look for the safe, the more I knew about it, the easier it would be. I was expecting to be looking for a wall safe. The house was dimly lit inside, and smelt as though no fresh air had entered in the last thirty years.

The first room I came to was a living room. It was tidier than I expected it to be, but very dusty; I guessed that Harper didn't spend much time in there. There was also a dining room; it had a large oak table, with one chair. I felt a little sad for him, living so alone, but it was his choice. Off the dining room was a large farmhouse kitchen, you could easily cook for a hundred people in that kitchen, yet there was only one plate and one glass on the side. I went back into the hallway and tried the door at the end; this was a study. There was a desk with papers all over it and there at the back of the room was an enormous free standing safe.

It was old and rusted in places, but it was a beauty. A Dottling, a luxury German brand. From its design and the state it was in I guessed it came from sometime in the 1940's. At that time Dottling were making some of the best safes in the world. Good old-fashioned combination lock. This was the sort you saw in movies, with the big dial on the front. I could see that it was a hundred digit dial, which was about standard for a safe this size.

I had cracked similar before, but never this model. They usually had a three to six digit combination. The good news was it wouldn't take many tools. The bad news was it might take some time. The thing with these safes was that they were shipped from the manufacturer with a try-out combination. This was usually a standard code, that all of the same model would use, it was not uncommon for people not to change the code. If I was lucky, I might be able to find the try-out combination through some of my contacts back in London. If old man Harper hadn't bothered to change the code, this would be easy. If he had, I'd have to try manipulating the lock. This method got the best results and left no damage to the lock. If I shut it back up after, it could be ages before Harper even knew he'd been robbed, by which time I would be long gone.

I considered getting started now, but when I looked at my watch I realised I only had fifteen minutes to go before Harper returned. It could wait a week.

God, it's so hot, and the crows, they are still laughing at me, their caws echoing across the field and into my ears. One of the fuckers just took a shit on my shoulder. If I could get my hands on them I would rip their bloody wings off, but I can't. I just have to wait. So thirsty. So very thirsty.

The following week, I parked my car a little nearer to Harper's farm, so I would be able to see him pull out of the drive in that Land Rover of his. Once he was around the bend, I would drive up and park outside the house. If there was really as much gold as Mickey Welby claimed, then I was not going to manage to carry it down the road to the car in the time I'd have when I'd got the safe open.

I'd put in a call to an old friend. I say friend. In the criminal world, you don't really have many of them. Most would willingly turn you in to save their own skin, so really he was more of an acquaintance. Among safecrackers, he was known as the professor due to his encyclopaedic knowledge of almost every safe ever made. He had plans for them, he had try-out codes for them, he even collected the bloody things and sold them as antiques. He was the go to man if you had a question about a particular safe.

'Well, fucking hell,' he said, in his thick Cockney accent. 'Everyone thought you were dead, mucker. No one's seen hide nor hair of you in months.'

'I decided to get out of the game,' I said. 'It all got a bit too intense after that job in Brixton.'

'Like I say to anyone who'll listen...' he started to say.

'Never work with the Garrety brothers,' I finished. 'They get the biggest jobs, though, plus I owed them a favour.'

'Yeah well, it's done now. Jimmy's dead and Phil's in prison for life,' the professor said.

'Yeah, I saw it in the paper. I knew they fell out over the money, but killing your own brother, what kind of psycho does that?'

'A Garrety,' the professor said. 'Their old man was just the same.'

We talked a little. I told him I was living in the country, not wanting to put him in the position of knowing too much about my whereabouts.

'So to what do I owe the pleasure of this call?' he said. 'I doubt you just phoned because you missed me did you?'

'I need a try out code,' I said. 'For a Dottling 1940's free stander.'

'I thought you'd gone straight,' he said chuckling to himself.'

'I'm going straight,' I said. 'This is the last job for me. It's one I can't refuse.'

'Well, have you got a model number?' He said.

'Yeah, it's a 126,' I replied.

'Bloody hell, make my life easy why don't you?' he said. 'There were about ten variations of that model in the 40's, each with its own try-out combination. You got a serial number?'

'No,' I said, kicking myself for not looking for it, though I knew they were usually underneath, which would have made it difficult to get to.

'Tell me more about it, what dial's it got?' The professor asked.

'Standard,' I said.

'Was there any decoration on the outside of it? Some of their safes are like works of art.'

'No,' I replied. 'It was just metal, rusty greenish grey metal.'

'Ah,' the professor said. 'Sounds like it was a military safe.'

He explained that he thought he might have the try-out combination for the safe, he would check and I should call him back in a few hours.

A slight breeze came across the field. It's caress was soothing on my sunbaked skin. It had picked up the faint aroma of spring flowers on its travels, the scent was sweet relief from the smell of my own sweat and the crow shit on my shoulder.

The crows now seemed to sit around me, their cold black eyes regarding me with sideways glances.

Could they sense how near the end I was? They cawed at each other as if in some great discussion over my fate.

I was reminded of some old wives tale I had heard years before, one that had been lurking in the back of my mind. It was about how crows were able to travel between the worlds of the living and the dead, and that they were responsible for transporting the souls from this world to the next. That was why they were here, as I waited to die, they waited to carry me to the next world. What lay in store for me there? I was a career criminal. I had spent my life stealing. If the Ten Commandments were true then surely I was destined for hell. Yet as the refreshing breeze subsided, and the sun continued to beat down on my battered, aching body, I was convinced I was already in hell. What came next had to be better.

The week after I had entered Harper's house for the first time, I sat in my car waiting for him to leave once more. On the passenger seat next to me sat my duffle bag, containing all of the tools I might feasibly need. I had a lock pick, just in case Harper had thought to lock his door today. I had my stethoscope, in case I had to try to manipulate the lock. I would be able to do it without but the stethoscope, but it would make life easier. I even had a drill and small amount of explosive. On the off chance that manipulation failed I would use these to blow the lock. Explosives were my least favourite way to work, though, there was no real artistry to it, any idiot could do it with a bit of practice. No, the real skill lay in lock manipulation. With this, you used your ears to listen for the distinctive clicks that told you which numbers made up the combination. This was what you would see in films, the safe cracker with his ear pressed to the safe turning the dial, then opening the safe. Of course, reality was much more complicated. You had to graph the point of convergence, where the clicks interlinked. This would show you which number made up the combination, but not the order, so you would have to try all of the different possible orders. With a simple three-digit combination, there were six possible combinations to try.

When I called the professor back, he gave me the good news, that most of that model of Dottling safe were only three number combinations, and that he also had the try-out combination, 6-82-12. If old man Harper had never bothered to change the combination, this was the only thing I would need.

I was anxious to get in and get started; it was always the same before a job. I wished I had a cigarette to smoke, that was always how I use to handle the pre match nerves as it were; however, I had quit just after I left London. So instead, I tapped nervously on the steering wheel, watching the clock. For the first time since I had been observing his habits, Harper was running late. It made me uneasy. I was a strong believer that if something felt wrong about a job you should just walk away, but how could I walk away from the potential life changing treasure in that safe? I couldn't, I had become obsessed with the idea of getting into the safe. Even if Mickey's story about the gold was utter shit, I still had to know what someone like Harper would keep in a safe.

Finally, ten minutes behind schedule, I saw Harper pulling out of the driveway in his dirt splattered Land Rover. He didn't seem to even glance in my direction, this was comforting as I had been worried that he would spot the car and become suspicious. Instead, he turned left and headed towards the village. As the Land Rover disappeared around the first, tree lined bend I started the engine and slowly drove up the road towards the entrance to Harper's farm.

I looked around for sign of any other vehicle, there were none around, so I headed up the driveway and pulled up outside the house. My heart was thumping in my chest as I got out of the car, and my palms were sweating inside my leather gloves. I was dressed all in black, with long sleeves, gloves and a beanie hat. The unseasonably hot weather had already begun, and a little sweat ran from under the hat and down into my eye. It stung like hell. I took off the beanie and wiped my eyes with it.

I took the duffle bag from the passenger seat and headed to the front door. As I had hoped, Harper had left it unlocked once more. I quickly headed to the study; time was, after all, of the essence. There it stood at the back of the room, swathed in shadows, my opponent, the safe. I rushed over and set the bag down at the side of the safe, I rubbed my hand over it. I don't know why I always did this. I just needed to feel its strength before I tried to crack a safe.

I pulled out the scrap of paper on which I had scrawled the try-out combination the professor had given me. I felt the dial. There was a stiffness to it that was unusual, this was often a sign that the safe had not been opened in some time, also it made manipulation more difficult. The stiffness of the dial caused its own creaks and clicks, these made the clicks of the wheels parking, difficult to discern.

I slowly turned the wheel, entering each digit of the try-out combination 6, then 82 and finally 12. I heard the most satisfying click a safe cracker can ever hear, the sound of the fence dropping into the grooves on the wheels and unblocking the locking pin. The combination had worked. Thank God for people too lazy to bother with changing a safe's combination. I went to open the heavy door of the safe.

I think the heat and dehydration were really starting to get to me. The heat beating down on me was finally driving me mad. I heard the crows cawing still, but I also heard words within the sounds. Words like thief, crook and bastard. The crows were judging me, those dead black eyes regarding me with the disdain of a jury convinced of my guilt. I wanted to scream, but of course I couldn't. I was only capable of the quietest mumble, thanks to Harper. One of the crows flew onto my shoulder. It cawed loudly, and then began to peck at my earlobe, it's powerful beak clamping down and easily breaking the skin. I did not mind, the pain was a distraction from the heat, and a reminder that I was still alive.

From the position of the sun, and the change in the tones of colour in the field, I guessed that it was about mid afternoon. I felt like my throat would crack open from thirst, it had been so long since my last ration of filthy water, but evening was coming and Harper would return soon.

Mickey Welby was a lying son of a bitch. I had pulled the heavy, and somewhat seized up, safe door open. I was not greeted by the sight of an impossible mountain of gold. Instead, there were dusty manila folders, some old photograph albums, and a single ingot of gold bullion. That was enough, though, at today's high gold prices that would be worth somewhere between four hundred grand and half a million. Admittedly I wouldn't be able to set myself up for life, but it would make life more comfortable.

I picked up the ingot and examined it. I almost dropped it when I saw the markings on the top. There, as clear as day, was a Swastika. This was Nazi gold. The historical significance could be worth a lot more to the right collector than the gold value. I tucked the Ingot into the duffle bag and flicked through the folders. Most of them were to do with the finances of the farm, which seemed to be quite successful. This came as a bit of a surprise as no one in the village even knew what exactly Harper grew up here, one rumour was that he was actually farming cannabis. The more boring reality was wheat mainly. Harper only hired in labourers from outside the area, and only at harvest time. It appeared he did everything else on the farm himself.

I continued flicking through the folders and found some papers that were written in what looked like German to me. This answered the question of old man Harper's country of origin.

Finally, I looked through the photograph album. There were a few old snaps of old man Harper and his bride on their wedding day, a few shots of them with the current Mr Harper as a baby, and he was surprisingly cute as a child. Growing up had not been kind to him.

After the few family shots and some holiday photos there was a gap in the album, but when I skipped a few pages I saw a photograph that sent a chill through me. It was clearly old man Harper in the picture, though in it he was far from old. He was a young, athletic, handsome man, who just happened to be wearing an SS officer's uniform.

The photograph explained the Nazi gold ingot and why Harper would change his name and lose his accent as quickly as possible. He was hiding.

All at once, I felt uneasy in the house, I couldn't explain the sensation, it just felt like I was invading in issues far bigger than myself. I put the album back in the safe and locked it back up. I zipped up my duffle bag and turned to leave the room.

Stood there blocking my path was the hulking frame of Harper. He looked at me with that same smile he had on his face the day he nearly ran me over. Too late, I noticed the lead pipe in his hand. He swung it at the side of my head. There was a moment of white-hot pain, and then blackness engulfed me.

The crow on my shoulder continued to peck at the soft tissue of my earlobe for a while. I could feel the warm, sticky trickle of blood that creeped lazily down the side of my neck. Then my avian attacker turned his attention to the stitches above my ear, and the raw flesh where Harper had hit me with the pipe. I could feel it ripping out the stitches that Harper had so carefully done to stop the bleeding. I felt the wound opening and the crow's beak exploring the inside of the wound. As he did this, his friends all stood around flapping their dirty, black angel wings and cawing, cheering him on like a ravenous pack of demons.

When I came to, I was strapped to a metal table. At first I felt disorientated, not quite sure of where I was. I knew that I was naked, and that the metal was cold against my flesh. I was in a room with no windows that felt cool and smelled ever so slightly damp. I was in a basement.

My head throbbed, like I'd been kicked by a mule. Then I saw Harper walking around in overalls.

'Ah, you're awake,' he said in a voice that I had not expected. He sounded much more refined and educated than his appearance would have led you to assume he was.

'Where?' it was all I could manage to say.

'Shh,' he said soothingly. 'You need to rest. I've stitched up the wound on your head. I didn't want you to bleed to death in my office.'

I was having trouble processing the information. Harper was the one who had hit me with the lead pipe. He had caused my injury. So why now was he showing all of this concern? Why hadn't he turned me over to the police?

'The police?' I asked.

'No,' he said. 'I haven't called them. You have been a very naughty boy, though, haven't you. Coming in here, rummaging through personal things, and trying to take things that aren't yours.'

He sounded like he was talking to a child. I was growing more frightened by the second.

'Let me go,' I said weakly.

He looked at me sadly and shook his head.

'I'm sorry, but I can't do that,' he said. 'You might tell some one about Daddy, about who he was. Mainly, though, you have to be punished for your behaviour. I can't let the police in here snooping around, not without them finding out the truth, so I'm going to have to punish you my own way.'

'No,' I said, struggling against the leather straps that held me to the metal table.

'Shh,' he said again softly. 'You're going to need your strength.'

He walked away from me and went over to a shelf. He opened a box and pulled out a syringe and a small bottle of clear fluid.

'I'm going to have to put you to sleep for a while now,' he said. 'Believe me when I say it's all for the best. You really wouldn't want to be awake for the next part.'

As he filled up the syringe, I screamed, louder than I had ever screamed in my life. I screamed for him to stop. I screamed for help. I screamed until my throat bled and my lungs hurt. It didn't help. Harper came over and stuck the syringe into a vein in my arm, and as I felt a pressure on my chest, the world slipped away.

When I came to this time, I could feel Harper was holding my hand.

'Listen to me very carefully,' he said gently. 'Do not try and open your eyes, and do not try and speak. If you do the pain will be terrible.'

I wanted to do both, yet I believed his warning.

'I want you to squeeze my hand once for yes, and twice for no, do you understand.'

I squeezed his hand once.

'Firstly, there is nothing wrong with your eyes, you will be able to see just fine when I get you out there. Secondly, your mouth is going to be very sore, you just have to try your hardest to keep it still. Do you understand?'

I squeezed his hand once more.

'Good, I'm going to leave you now to rest for the night, but tomorrow morning your punishment starts. Do you understand?'

I squeezed his hand once more.

'Good,' he said. 'I'm going to put a small tube into your nose. This is just to keep you hydrated overnight; it's just a saline solution like you would have in hospital. Tomorrow morning I will feed you through the tube.'

He inserted the tube through my nose and down into my stomach. Then he left me alone in the darkness.

The next time I woke up, I could see. Whatever had been covering my eyes had been removed. I saw Harper stood there in front of me. He was removing the saline drip that had been going through the tube in my nose. He took the end of the tube and attached it to a large syringe, containing some brown substance.

He looked down and noticed I was awake. He smiled at me.

'Good morning,' he said cheerfully, I hope you're not in too much pain, I gave you some tramadol in the night, it might mean you're still a little woozy.'

I tried to tell him that I was, but I felt a sharp pain in my lips. I couldn't open my mouth.

'Shh,' he said. 'Don't try and speak, I've stitched your lips together. I've only left enough of a gap for you to breathe if your nose gets blocked.'

I must have been dreaming. This had to be some kind of surreal nightmare, where the monster seemed so caring and gentle while inflicting such hideous torments upon me. I thrashed around against the straps, banging my head repeatedly against the metal table. Harper ignored it; he carried on connecting the tube in my nose to the syringe.

'This is food,' he said. 'I'm pumping it straight into your stomach through the tube in your nose. It contains all of the nutrients you need for a day. It won't stop you feeling hungry, but it'll stop you dying of malnutrition.'

I gave up thrashing, there was no point, there was no escape. My only hope was that whatever punishment Harper had in mind for me, it would be over quickly.

That was two weeks ago. I've spent every hour since then nailed to this cross in this field, a human scarecrow, except I do not scare them, they taunt me. I am a useless scarecrow.

I have seen cars drive by, but they do not stop. Why would they? All they see is a scarecrow in a field. There is nothing out of the ordinary in that around here. On a few occasions people have walked past the field, walking their dogs. Of course, I can't open my mouth to scream, and I'm too well fixed to the cross to show them I'm alive through movement. So I just stay here, day and night, sun and rain. My only company is the crows, and they hate me,

Harper comes twice a day, once in the morning, and once in the evening. He inserts the tube into my nose and feeds me and gives me water. He gives me enough to survive, but not enough to stop suffering.

I am serving my sentence. Harper says that if I survive until harvest he will let me go, I want to believe him. The thing is I don't know if I can survive that long. It is months until harvest. The crows will have driven me mad a long time before then. I think they have already.

FEAR THY NEIGHBOUR

Timmy looked out of his window and saw the old man, Mr Phelps, looking up at him. Timmy did not like Mr Phelps at all. He was scared of him. The old man lived in the house next door all on his own. Mummy said that Timmy was being silly, that Mr Phelps was just a lonely and nosy old man, but Timmy knew better. Mr Phelps would stand out there on his front porch staring up at Timmy's house, staring at Timmy, for hours on end.

Mummy had spoken to Mr Phelps a few times when they had first moved into the house, three months back. Mr Phelps had knocked on the door that first evening and introduced himself; Mummy had done the same. Timmy had hidden upstairs, peeking down and listening to them talk. The old man's voice was deep and rasping. It frightened Timmy; it reminded him of the way the bad man had spoken.

'So there's just you and yer boy?' Mr Phelps had asked.

'Yes, that's right,' Mummy had answered. 'His father left sometime ago.'

Daddy had left after the bad man had taken Timmy, after Timmy had gotten sick. Mummy said that Daddy was not a bad man, he just didn't know how to deal with what had happened, that he had been unable to protect his son.

Mummy was sick, too, Timmy had given her the disease. She didn't blame him, though, it was after the bad man had taken him and done the vile things to him. The bad man had the sickness and passed it onto Timmy when he did the bad thing to him. There was no way they could have known he was poorly when he got home, covered in blood and bruises. Mummy had cleaned his wounds up, but she had a cut on her hand, and that was how she had gotten sick, too. The sickness scared Timmy; he would often cry himself to sleep worrying about dying. Mummy would come in and comfort him, saying that they both had a long time before they had to worry about that. Timmy was not so sure, though. Who could know how long they would have?

They had lived in the city then and Timmy had gone to school, but that had all changed now. They now lived on the edge of a small village in the countryside. Their house and Mr Phelps' were the only two around for some distance. Timmy didn't like being so far away from other people, especially with the way that Mr Phelps looked at him like he wanted to hurt him, like the bad man.

Timmy didn't go to school anymore. Mummy taught him at home. She was afraid that if she sent him to school then the other children would learn about him being poorly, and they wouldn't understand. So they would sit in the living room and Mummy would teach him to do sums and read books and everything else he did at school anyway. Sometimes Mummy got frustrated with him, because he was a slow learner. He never used to be, before the bad man took him. Since then, though, he had found it increasingly hard to concentrate, things would not sink in the way they used to. Mummy would shout at him for getting things wrong, then she would cry and hug him tight and tell him she was sorry.

Tomorrow was Timmy's birthday. Mummy had promised him that she would take him out for dinner and they would go to the cinema. He loved going to the cinema more than anything. Mummy kissed him goodnight and he went up to his room. He was changing into his pyjamas when he saw Mr Phelps stood on his porch looking up at him. He just stood there smoking his stinky pipe and watching Timmy get changed. Timmy knew the look on his face; it was the same one the bad man had when he did the bad thing to him. Timmy pulled his thick, heavy curtains shut and ran downstairs.

'I thought you were going to sleep?' Mummy said. 'It's your big day tomorrow.'

'Mr Phelps was watching me,' he said.

'Oh don't be silly,' Mummy said.

'He wants to hurt me.'

'No, he doesn't,' Mummy said. 'He's just a lonely old man. No one is going to hurt you ever again. I won't let them.'

She held him close to her, then patted his bottom.

'Now go to sleep.'

Timmy went back to his room and laid down, he couldn't sleep. His mind kept racing with a thousand thoughts. He remembered his Daddy, happy times of them playing together in the park. He thought about what he and Mummy would do the next day, what they would have to eat, and what the film would be like. These were all happy thoughts. He knew that they would go somewhere quiet to eat; Mummy didn't like to eating in crowded places. Then they would drive the fourteen miles to Lincoln to go to the cinema.

The image of Mr Phelps staring up at him kept popping back into his head and filling him with fear. Then he would remember the bad man, the way he had looked at Timmy as he walked home that winter evening. He remembered how he had just grabbed him, so strong, and carried him away. Then there was his foul smell, the thought of it made Timmy feel sick, and of course the pain.

Eventually he fell asleep, only to be woken by a loud banging on the front door. It was a furious thumping that scared him. He heard Mummy moving around downstairs, heading for the door. He wanted to scream at her not to open it, to come and hide with him, but the words would not come. Instead, all he could do was silently creep to the top of the stairs and watch in horror as the scene unfolded before him.

The banging on the door continued, getting heavier and faster. Mummy stepped in the hallway.

'Just a minute,' she said cheerfully, as though the force of the knocking was nothing unusual. How could she not be afraid? It was as if whoever was outside was trying to hammer their way into the house. Of course Timmy knew who was outside, Mr Phelps.

Mummy opened the door, and sure enough there stood the old man from next door. He seemed bigger standing in the doorway than he ever had when Timmy had seen him through the window. He stood there with his hands behind his back. Mummy looked startled to see him, but acted friendly enough.

'Mr Phelps,' she said. 'Is everything all right?'

Mr Phelps didn't answer, he just stood there silently looking at Mummy, and then his eyes moved slowly up the staircase. He met Timmy's gaze. Timmy was so scared that he darted his head back into his room.

'Mr Phelps,' he heard Mummy say. 'Is there something I can help you with?'

There was no reply. Timmy looked back through the door carefully, just peeking out enough to see. Mr Phelps was still just standing motionless in the doorway, his hands behind his back. Mummy was starting to look annoyed.

'Mr Phelps, I don't mean to be rude, but if there's nothing I can do for you, then I'm sorry but I'm a little busy at the moment.'

A strange smile crossed the old man's face. Timmy didn't like it. It seemed full of hate and evil, like the bad man.

Mummy began to shut the door, but Mr Phelps shot out one of his arms and held it open, that sinister smile still on his face.

'Mr Phelps, let me shut my door please,' Mummy said. She was starting to sound cross.

'No,' the old man said in a rumbling tone that filled Timmy with dread. 'It's time.'

'Time for wha...' Mummy began to say, but before she could finish Mr Phelps lifted his other arm from behind his back. He was holding a long knife, Timmy thought it was called a machete, but he wasn't sure.

Mr Phelps lunged at Mummy with the knife raised high, the blade hurtling through the air towards her. She was more agile, though, and managed to sidestep the attack. Mr Phelps fell through the door, crashing to the floor. Mummy looked up the stairs and met Timmy's terrified gaze.

'Timmy, hide!' she shouted up.

He wanted to, really he did, he wanted to find somewhere safe to curl up and make all of this go away, but he couldn't. He was frozen to the spot in fear, unable to stop watching the terrible things happening before him.

Mummy tried to step over the lump on the floor that was Mr Phelps and get to the stairs. Mr Phelps, though, had other ideas. His hand shot out and pulled on Mummy's ankle. She screamed as she fell to the floor. They struggled on the floor; Mummy was hitting the old man, clawing at his face and even trying to bite him, something she'd told Timmy he must never do.

Mr Phelps was too strong, though, he pinned her down and then brought the blade down hard into Mummy's chest. She looked up at Timmy, blood seeping from her mouth, her eyes full of pain and fear.

'Run,' she managed to rasp.

Mr Phelps looked up directly at Timmy; his face was covered in Mummy's blood. He smiled up at Timmy. The paralysis of fear was broken and Timmy was up on his feet. He wanted to run out of the house, but knew there was no way that he could get past Mr Phelps without the murderous old man catching him. Instead, he ran to Mummy's room. He knew there was a built-in wardrobe that had a shelved area at the back that he would be able to fit in. Mr Phelps would be able to find him easily, but Timmy hoped that the old man would not be able to reach him back there. As he began to run towards Mummy's room, he heard the thunderous footfalls of the old man running up the stairs. Timmy had never felt so scared in his life, not even when the bad man had taken him. At least the bad man had told him that if Timmy let him do what he wanted without fighting, then he would not kill him. Timmy knew that was exactly what Mr Phelps wanted to do. He wanted to kill him just like he had killed Mummy.

He flew into Mummy's room, not even bothering to shut the door behind him; it would take more time than he had. Mr Phelps was quick for his age and was almost right behind him. Timmy ran to the wardrobe and pulled open the door. Turning back, he saw Mr Phelps entering the room. Timmy crouched down and went to climb into the space under the shelves. To his horror, he saw that the space was full of boxes wrapped in colourful paper. His birthday presents.

Mr Phelps grabbed him by the ankles and pulled him out of the wardrobe. He looked down at Timmy with that same dark smile.

'It's time,' he said.

Timmy saw the blade coming down towards his chest and screamed.

Then darkness.

He was aware of the sound of his own screaming in the darkness.

Then the sound of Mummy's voice.

'Timmy, what's wrong?' she said as she came into the room. Even under his cover he could see the light come to life. Mummy pulled his cover off him and pulled him to her.

'Mr Phelps!' Timmy said through hysterical tears. 'He killed you and tried to kill me.'

Mummy stroked his hair.

'I'm right here, baby, no one has killed me, no one's going to,' she said soothingly. 'It was just a bad dream.'

'It seemed so real,' Timmy sobbed.

'No one is ever going to hurt you, or me. As long as we're careful,' she said.

She sat there holding him for some time, until his sobs had near enough subsided, then she gently lowered him back down.

'I love you, Mummy,' Timmy said, feeling himself getting sleepy again.

'I love you, too,' she said, planting a little kiss on his forehead with her cool lips. 'Now sleep tight, it's your 130th birthday tomorrow.'

Timmy smiled.

Mummy smiled, her perfect white fangs glinting as she did, nothing like the horrible, yellow and stained things the bad man had.

Mummy gently closed the lid of his coffin as Timmy drifted off into a peaceful sleep.

COFFIN HALL

The village of Cofnin laid ten miles southeast of the city of Lincoln. It was a picturesque little village, the local council had insisted that any house built there fit in with the style of the village, so even the new build house were all made of the same sandstone. The village had several countryside walks that encompassed woods, lakes, fields, pubs and the old hall.

Cofnin Hall had once been the home of Sir Andrew Mayler and his family. It had been built in the early nineteenth century and had served as home to the Mayler family for four generations, until the family ran into financial trouble and were forced to sell the house in the early twentieth century. The house was bought by the Government. Originally, they used it as an office for the Ministry of Agriculture, to oversee all of the work they had to do in the county.

During the Second World War, the house was handed over to the military. It was used as a hospital, treating airmen injured in operations over Germany, and also used to treat soldiers sent back from the front line.

The military kept hold of it until the late 1960's, at which point the house was sold to the national trust. They kept it open as a museum until someone decided to burn the place down in the mid eighties.

The fire ravaged the building. Though it still stood, the damage to the roof and floors throughout was far too expensive for the trust to consider restoring. So for the last thirty years, the hall has sat abandoned and ruined, surrounded by its overgrown gardens and the woodlands that ever encroached on it. Weeds now grew inside the once great hall, and vines had devoured several walls inside and out.

With its dereliction came the reputation of the hall being haunted and the punning nickname Coffin Hall.

Local kids used it to prove their bravery, or to scare their friends, but for one girl investigating Coffin Hall was very serious indeed. That girl was Laura Green. For the last two years, Laura had spent almost every night searching the hall, desperate to find a ghost.

This night was no different. As Laura walked up the winding drive that led to the hall the sun was starting to set. It was late autumn and there was a fine rain in the air, but that didn't bother Laura. The house would be wet inside, but there were still some parts that offered shelter from the elements.

The previous night she had left some things behind, a few little experiments. She had written on the wall in chalk. A simple message, 'Are you there?' She had left the chalk on the floor near the message, hoping that tonight she would fine some sort of reply. It was of course always possible that someone living had found the message and decided to reply as a joke, but she hoped that she would be able to tell the difference.

She had heard all of the stories about the hall, and knew full well that most of them were rubbish. Supposedly, the ghost of a soldier who had died on the operating table in the hall when it was a hospital roamed the corridors at night looking for revenge on the surgeon who let him die.

Laura had done her research, though; she knew that it never had an operating theatre. It had triage, but most of the care that was done there was about recovery, not treatment. People who needed surgery were sent off to other hospitals.

There were stories, too, that Sir Andrew Mayler haunted the house. His anguished spirit was supposed to be in eternal torment, as his murderer had never been brought to justice. The problem was that Andrew Mayler died of natural causes at the age of eighty-seven; there was never any suggestion of murder.

Some of the stories about the house had some element of truth. There was supposed to be the ghost of a young boy, about eight years old, who had drowned in the pond in the grounds. He was supposed to search the house, looking endlessly for his mother.

Laura had found out that a boy of that age named Joseph Mayler, one of Sir Andrew's grandsons, had died in the pond in the garden. This gave some validity to the claims people made of seeing him. Apparently, he was always soaked to the skin. One of the few hints of a ghost that Laura had encountered within Coffin Hall was a single, small, wet footprint in one of the upstairs corridors.

There was also a story about a shell-shocked soldier who had hung himself from the beams in the ceiling of the great hall. Legend said that his spirit could be seen still hanging from the noose. Though Laura had never seen the dangling ghost on any of her many visits to the hall, she had found documents pertaining to the suicide of the soldier, so she supposed it was possible his spirit was there.

Also, there was supposed to be the spirit of a sad woman dressed all in white who was often seen upstairs, in the servants' quarters, wailing in despair. This could be the ghost of one of the maids for the

Mayler family. She had fallen pregnant. Rumour had it that the father was one of the Mayler family, but the baby was stillborn. Unable to overcome her grief, she, too, had committed suicide, by jumping from the roof of the hall.

The most recent ghost that Laura knew about was the ghost of a young woman who had been killed when one of the walls of the ruined house had collapsed on her. This had been all over the papers a few years ago.

Laura came to the hall as often as she could, spending whole nights there on occasions, desperate to see one of the spirits with her own eyes. It had started when her father died, she wanted some evidence of a life after death as this would give her some comfort. In recent years, though, the Hall, and hunting for its spectral occupants, had become something of an obsession.

It was a Friday night and that meant that there was always the chance of her being disturbed in her investigation. Local kids wanting to test their nerve, or just mess around, often came at the weekends, as did drunk adults who really should have known better. She hated it if they saw her; they always wanted to know who she was and what she was doing there. So she had taken to hiding away when she encountered other people in the hall.

The first thing she did was to check the wall where she had written the message. The rain of earlier in the day had managed to run down the wall a little, fading her question, but it was still legible, 'Are you there?' She looked on the ground for the piece of chalk she had left. It was still there, but she could have sworn that she had left it under the word 'Are', but now it rested under the question mark at the end of the sentence. She looked back up at the wall; there was something, a white smudge of chalk. She peered at it, trying to see if there was some semblance of a letter or a word there. It was no use. If there had been any kind of intelligent meaning behind it, it had been washed away by the rain. For all she knew it could have been an answer from a spirit, or a joke from a living person, or just some of the chalk that had run off of her own message.

Disheartened, she moved to the great hall. The roof on this part of the hall was still intact, and the beams remained in the ceiling. One of them was the beam that the shell-shocked soldier had hung himself from. In here, she had lined three stones up on the floor and left a fourth nearby, hoping that one of the spirits would complete the pattern.

The stones were all scattered. Perhaps a spirit had been annoyed at her wanting it to play games, or perhaps someone living had walked through and moved the stones by accident. This was not evidence.

She heard it clearly, footsteps echoing through the ruin of the hall. She ran out of the great hall and stood at the foot of the enormous staircase. She tried to determine whether the sound was coming from upstairs or down here. She listened intently, for a moment she thought the footsteps had stopped, then she heard them again. The sound was definitely coming from above. She carefully climbed the staircase, some of the steps were rotten and it was easy to fall through if you stepped in the wrong place. When she reached the top of the stairs, she stopped and listened once more.

Again, the sound had disappeared. Laura wondered if one of the spirits was playing with her. Then it started up again, it was coming from the corridor that led to the east side of the house. This is where the nursery and children's bedrooms had been when it was a family home. Was this the ghost of the drowned boy, Joseph Mayler? She set off down the corridor, hoping that she would see something. The light in the corridor was quite good, the streetlights shone through the windows, upstairs they were not boarded up, and the moon shone brightly through the gaps in the roof.

It was a few years ago that she had a similar experience to this. She had heard the footsteps from downstairs and followed the sound down this same corridor. It was that night that she had found the wet footprint. It was right in the middle of the corridor on one of the floorboards, a small but perfectly formed footprint left in water. A child had obviously left it due to the size, and whoever had made it had been barefoot. The print was so clear that she could even see the small toe prints.

She was ashamed of the fact that she had run away that night, the shock of the print instigated an instinctual reaction and she had fled the house. It was that primeval fear of the unknown; it had taken over her and made her run. She had kicked herself later for giving in to such fear, but by the time she returned the print, and the sound of footsteps, had gone, and she had never encountered it again.

Now, though, the footsteps were back, walking the same corridor as that night. Was she about to find another wet footprint? If so, she would not run this time. This time she would stay and continue looking for the ghost of the drowned boy; she would try to communicate with him. Of course, she realised quickly that there was no hope of seeing a wet footprint this time. Though the night was clear and moonlit now, it had been raining all day. The wooden boards of the corridor were sodden with water.

Suddenly she heard another sound. It sounded like a whisper. It came from the room at the end of the corridor; this had been the nursery once upon a time. She stopped in her tracks and waited. She was starting to think she had imagined the sound when it came again, a clear sound of a human voice, a young human voice, whispering. Laura felt that same desire to run that she had experienced before, but this time she controlled it, she was determined. She quietly glided down the corridor towards the nursery. The whispering continued. When she reached the doorway, the door itself was long gone, she carefully peeked around it into the room. This side of the house was less well lit, as it faced away from the streetlights, but there was enough moonlight coming in for her to make out shapes, and after a few moments peering in her eyes began to adjust and everything became clearer.

At first, she saw nothing. The room appeared completely still. Then she heard the whisper again, and when she looked in the direction it came from she spotted a small figure in the room. She felt herself being overcome with emotion. The figure looked a little to tall to be an eight-year-old boy, though. Then she saw the second figure. They were stood next to each other looking out of the window. They whispered to each other in hushed tones, but from here she could make out the words.

'It's really creepy,' the smaller figure said. 'Can we go now?'

'Don't be a wimp,' said the slightly larger figure. 'I want to see a ghost.'

Laura felt utterly disappointed. They weren't ghosts. They were just local kids, in here looking to be scared. She didn't want to get into a conversation with them. She wanted to be left alone in the house to continue her investigation. She decided to slip back downstairs and wait for them to leave. She moved away from the door. Rather than walk back along the long corridor, she headed to the door that led to the servants' staircase. As she made her way to the door, she felt her foot go down too hard on a very damp floorboard. The board snapped in half with a loud crack. Laura let out a little surprised scream and fell to the floor with a thud.

A loud, terrified scream came from the nursery. Obviously the kids had heard the noise she had made. They ran out of the room and saw her sprawled on the floor trying to get up. The fear in their eyes was amazing. Without saying a word to her, they ran back along the corridor. She heard their hurried steps all the way to and down the staircase.

She picked herself up and guessed that she once more had the house to herself. The hope she had felt when she heard the whispers and first saw the figure in the nursery had been overwhelming, and now that it had turned out just to be a couple of kids she felt utterly devastated.

Normally she would stay in the house until the sky outside started to lighten, but after that disappointment, she had had enough for the night.

Slowly, she made her way back towards the main staircase. Her mood was low, she considered writing another chalk message for the spirits, but then thought what was the point?

She left Coffin Hall by the main entrance. As she walked back along the gravel driveway, she stopped and looked back at the ruined mansion. Were there any spirits in there? If so, would she ever find them? She carried on walking away from the hall, her mind swirling with thoughts that she was wasting her time.

She crossed the street and walked through the churchyard. She thought to herself that maybe she should give up her quest. It had started as a way to prove that there was an afterlife. She wanted to know that it was possible that her father lived on somewhere, but surely, she had enough proof of that now. It was after the accident that she had started going to the hall more and more often, no longer looking for proof.

She stopped and looked at a grave. A tear came to Laura's eye when she saw the fresh flowers lent against the headstone. Her mother had been to the grave recently. Laura remembered the pain of her father's death, and the agony of the wall in Coffin Hall collapsing on her, crushing her to death. Now both of their bodies were laid side by side in the churchyard.

Laura no longer needed proof that ghosts were real. Her own continued existence was proof enough. Now she searched the hall night after night for others like her. She was so very lonely.

WHAT GROWS IN THE FAR FIELD

David Barker was in trouble. Not the 'this is going to cause a few problems' kind of trouble, no, David was in the 'heading straight up shit creek without a paddle' kind of trouble. The way he saw it, he had less than three weeks before everything fell apart. Less than three weeks until those bastards at the bank came and took it all away from him. Not only would he lose his business, but also his home and the legacy of his family.

Hardwick Farm had been in David's family for nearly a hundred and fifty years. His great, great, great grandfather had founded it in 1864. Thomas Hardwick had put his heart and soul into getting the farm and his blood, sweat and tears into making it a success.

It had passed down the line from oldest son to oldest son, until that is David's grandfather, Maurice Hardwick. Maurice only had one daughter Jean Hardwick, who went on to marry David's father John Barker. The two of them ran the farm, and when they retired, it was left to David.

It had not all been his fault. David had done all of the things he should have done. He went to university and studied agricultural management, gained a first class honours degree in fact. Plus, he had spent almost his whole life on this bloody farm, he knew how everything worked, or at least how it was supposed to work. He had just had a run of bad luck. Three years ago, half of his farm land had flooded, destroying all of the crops that had been growing in them. What he managed to save was barely enough to cover paying his workers. The following year, his entire potato crop had got blight. The disease had ravaged his crops, making them useless. Last year his entire wheat crop had failed. His land was becoming dead, unable to grow the simplest thing.

He looked out on his fields. This year's crop looked like it would be a no go as well. He had sown the seeds nearly a month ago, and there wasn't even the slightest hint of them sprouting. It was no use, his life as a farmer was over and his family legacy would belong to the bank within the month.

He looked at the sun setting over his barren fields. The sky was burning red. Red sky at night, the bank gets your farm. He laughed, a sad little chuckle to try and hide his despair, even from himself. He headed into the farmhouse. He needed to eat something, even though he hadn't felt hungry in weeks, but more importantly, he needed a drink.

He made himself some beans on toast, but most of it went in the bin. He would fill up on whiskey, he decided. He pulled the half a bottle of Jameson out of the cupboard and sat down in front of the TV.

He wasn't watching it, really. It was just noise, some sense of company. He found himself getting increasingly lonely of late. His wife Tanya had left him nearly a year ago, though things had not been going well for years before that. At first, he had enjoyed the freedom. After all, they had been together since they were in their teens. At forty-one, he had found it incredibly easy to adjust to single life. He would spend most nights in the village pub, and then at weekends he would head into town, checking out the bars and clubs. There had been a few girls, though none of them were much more than one night stands.

Lately, though, he had been feeling the isolation more and more. Part of it was the money worries. He had no one he could talk them through with, no one to tell him that everything would be alright. He called his parents once a week, and on a few occasions he had nearly confided in his mother; her gentle tone was so reassuring, but he always stopped himself. Why should he worry them, too? They had sunk all of their money into the house in Spain and were spending there remaining days in moderate luxury. How could he confess that he had all but lost everything they had worked for, everything her entire family had worked for.

The whiskey was soon down to less than a quarter. He didn't bother with a glass, choosing to simply swig it straight from the bottle. It numbed the worry a little, never completely, but at least enough to allow him to sleep. Once he felt that warm, comforting numbness over come him, he headed up to bed, his big, cold, lonely bed.

He lay in bed a little while, thinking things through. There was no way he could get another loan from the bank. He was still paying back the one he took out last year, when things started heading south. He had no close friends anymore, or at least none who he could ask for the sort of money he needed. He began to think that perhaps if a fire were to destroy some of his out buildings and machinery, he might just get enough from the insurance to keep the farm ticking over for a few more months. If he prayed hard enough, perhaps God would hear him, and his crops would start to grow.

He fell into an alcohol-inspired sleep. His dreams were dark and confusing. He dreamt of Tanya, of strangling the life out of her. Then he dreamt of his mother, crying over the loss of the farm. He dreamt of looking up from his own grave as his father tossed a handful of dirt down on his face.

He heard the noises at first still in a dream, it sounded to him like farm machinery, only much larger and more powerful than anything he had ever heard before. It made no sense in the dream as he dreamt that he had destroyed all of his machinery. For a moment, he thought that the tractors, threshers and harvesters had returned for their revenge on him.

All at once, he was awake and aware that the noise was not only real, but deafening. Blinding lights shone through his bedroom window, sweeping across and then back again. First bright white, then red, then white once more. It was so bright that it made his head pound unless he shielded his eyes with his arm.

He virtually fell out of bed, rolling onto the hardwood floor. He crawled with his eyes shut in the direction of the door. He reached up, fumbling, for the door handle. In panic and the post drunken haze, it took him several attempts to locate it. Finally, he felt the cool metal in his hand and pulled it down. He dragged himself out onto the landing and slammed the door shut behind him. He rolled onto his back and laid there for a moment panting from the effort. The noise was still loud out here, but not quite as deafening, and the lights were barely visible from the landing window.

His bedroom faced north, and the landing window faced west. As his wits came back to him, he realised that someone was on his land. Most of his fields were off to the east and west. The only things to the north were his barns, the warehouses and the far field. He could not understand what was making all of the noise, but convinced himself that someone was trying to steal his machinery. He knew from experience that the lights on the harvester were brighter than the sun.

Earlier he had thought about torching all of the machinery himself to claim on the insurance, but that would be his own doing, and he was damned if he was going to let someone steal from him. It was just adding insult to injury. He was going to get his gun and confront the bastards head on.

He was pretty much fully clothed, as he was most nights these days. He still had his keys in his trouser pocket. He got to his feet and raced down the hall to the gun cabinet he kept in the spare room. The lock always seemed to stick, and in his current state, it took him a while to get it unlocked. He pulled out the shotgun, it was not something he used very often. Occasionally he would use it to take a pot shot at a fox trying to get at his chickens. Other than that, though, it mostly sat there in the cabinet. It had been his father's, maybe even his grandfather's, originally. He quickly loaded two cartridges into the gun and rand down the stairs.

He started to head for the kitchen, as the back door faced north and would allow him to see what was going on quicker, but then he remembered his boots were by the front door, and he was not heading outside barefoot.

He ran through the hall and grabbed his work boot. He tried pulling them on while standing. This was impossible however whilst holding the gun. He set the firearm down against the wall, carefully as it was loaded, and pulled on his boots. He was about to pick the gun up again when he noticed something out of place. On the doormat lay a white envelope that he was certain had not been there before. The post only came once a day, and he had picked his mail, mostly final reminders, up earlier that day. He left the gun where it was for a moment and bent down and picked up the envelope. His name was clearly written on the front, in some of the finest hand writing he had ever seen. There was no address written below it, the letter had been delivered by hand. He could not explain why he didn't just ignore it and continue investigating the disturbance outside, he just had an overwhelming sense that he should open it.

He ripped the envelope open, noticing the feel of the paper. It felt heavier than a normal envelope, and more metallic, kind of like one you would receive a birthday card in, only heavier. He slid out the single, neatly folded sheet of paper that was inside. The paper felt the same as the envelope. He unfolded it and read the message written in the same fine script.

Your crops will grow quicker and stronger than ever before. This is our gift to you and will solve all of your problems. What grows in the far field is not for you. You MUST stay out of there.

There was no signature, but it was clear that whoever sent the note was responsible for the noise and lights outside. He did not know what they were doing, but thieves did not leave you personally addressed notes. Whoever was out there, and whatever they were doing, they knew his name and that he had problems. Something about this unnerved him and made him not want to go out there and confront them. He kicked off his boots once more and took the note and the gun into the living room. He sat on the sofa. The lights were not too bad in this room, but the noise was still deafening. He picked up the whiskey bottle he had left in the room earlier and took a large gulp of it; its burn was comforting. David did not sleep that night, he sat on the sofa, listening to the roaring and swooshing of machinery he could not imagine. He drank the rest of the bottle of whiskey and cradled the loaded shotgun in his lap.

As the sun began to rise, at around six, the sound of machinery ceased. David had finished the whiskey, and as the morning light crept through the window, he drifted off into a deep sleep.

He woke up feeling hungover at about eleven in the morning. The loaded shotgun was still in his arms. It took him a few seconds to remember why it was there. He wondered if it had all been some kind of alcohol-induced hallucination at first. After all, he had been hitting the bottle hard lately, but then he saw the note laying next to him on the sofa. If that was real, he guessed that the rest must have been, too.

He went upstairs and locked the gun back up in the cabinet. Last night it may have made him feel more comfortable. In the cold light of day, however, it made him feel very unsafe having a loaded gun lying around. He washed and changed, then went to the kitchen and made himself a strong cup of coffee. He felt sober now, but knew there would still be a lot of the whiskey in his system.

He looked out of the kitchen window. From this vantage point nothing looked amiss, but from here the view of the far field was completely obscured by the barns and warehouses. Everything looked in order with them, so he decided to finish his coffee and then take a walk up to the far field.

When he got outside, he was surprised by how bright it was, but guessed that his hangover was making him a little over sensitive to the light. He wandered across his courtyard, stopping at several of the outbuildings to check their locks were in place and untampered with. They were all fine, even on the machine sheds; whatever the people who had sent the note were doing out there the previous night, they had not been trying to steal his property.

As he rounded the corner of his last barn, he saw something that should not have been there. Normally the far field was only accessible by its southern most edge; each of the other edges was surrounded by a dense copse. That morning however, the entire southern edge of the field was covered by a twenty foot high metal fence. It was enormous and solid. David could not see into the field at all. He walked over to the fence cautiously. It shone in the sunlight like chrome. He could see no break in it, no gate, no way of accessing the field at all. He gingerly outstretched his arm and ran his fingertips over the surface of the metal. It felt cold, and also like it was vibrating ever so slightly.

He walked along the length of the southern edge, following the fence. He found not a sign of a way of entering the field. When he came to the copse, he decided he would walk through there to see if the fence continued.

Following the field's perimeter through the rough terrain of the overgrown woodland took him thirty-seven minutes. The giant metal fence continued all the way around the field, totally cutting it off from the world. Though there had been points on the trip round that he had to veer slightly further away from the fence, to avoid trees and shrubs, he had tried to inspect it as closely as possible. Its surface appeared to be perfectly smooth, and as far as he had been able to see, had no entrances anywhere on it. Whoever had erected it would need either a very large ladder or a helicopter to get them inside.

David had a ladder back at the house, if he remembered rightly he had left it leaning against the front wall, from when he was cleaning the guttering out the other week. It was a long wooden one, and he was sure that it would at the very least get him high enough to look over and see what the hell was going on.

He rushed back to the house. Not wanting to waste time walking around it, he entered the house through the kitchen door and walked straight up the hall to the front door. When he got outside, he was about to turn right to where the ladder was propped up, but something stopped him in his tracks. His largest field, the south field, lay directly in front of his house. He always planted his wheat there, he made more money from the potatoes in the west field and the Brussels sprouts in the east field. They were very ugly plants, though, and he loved looking out of the window on a sunny day and seeing the golden wheat swaying in waves of breeze. This year, however, the seeds had not taken. In the month since he had sown them there had not been a trace of anything growing, until that morning.

Overnight, the wheat had sprouted and grown about eight inches. That sort of growth would normally take weeks, yet this had happened in the space of one night.

He remembered the words of the note. *Your crops will grow quicker and stronger than ever before. This is our gift to you.* The builders of the fence had not been lying about that part. He looked at the wooden ladder propped against wall of the farmhouse, and the rest of the note sprang to mind. *What grows in the far field is not for you. You MUST stay out of there.* There was something about the capitalisation of the word *MUST*, the emphasis they obviously intended to convey. If they had not been lying about their 'gift' to him, perhaps he was best to heed the warning, at least for the time being.

The wheat continued to grow at the same increased rate. Not only that, so, too, did his potato crop and the sprouts. If you looked first thing in the morning, the plants would have doubled in size by the evening. Within in a week David had to hire in teams of labourers to help him harvest the crops. From nothing to harvest in a week, this was an astounding reward for giving up his smallest field.

The unseasonal nature of the harvest was not unnoticed by some of the hired men. They asked him how he had managed to get the crops to grow so early. He lied and said that he was trying a new technique involving sowing earl and using different fertilisers. Most of them seemed to buy his story, and those that didn't were just happy to be receiving a good wage at such an unusual time of the year.

He sold his crops, feeding the buyers the same new technique story. He assured them that it was an all natural process, and that the produce tasted better than ever before. The buyers with an eye for profit accepted this and gladly bought his crop.

As soon as the harvest was over, David planted another crop in each of his three remaining fields, the next morning the seeds had begun to sprout. He was convinced that by the end of that week he would be able to do another harvest, he would have to hire in completely different labourers and sell to different buyers in order to avoid awkward questions, but this second crop would solve all of his money problems. It would save the farm. The loss of the far field really was a small price to pay, well, that and the loss of sleep.

Every night the noises and lights returned, with the deafening sound of machinery and the blinding bright lights. He had given up even trying to sleep in his bedroom, it was just impossible with the lights. Instead, he had moved into his parents' old room at the front of the house. With the door shut, this room offered some respite from the lights, but little from the noise. He tried wearing earplugs, but they were uncomfortable and only seemed to remove some of the higher frequency noises, not the low rumbles and thuds.

Most nights he sat awake, reading or watching TV with the subtitles on, trying to block out the incessant sound of machinery. Each night, though, as the sun rose, the sounds would cease. It was only then that David managed to get a little sleep, but with so much to do in the fields, he couldn't allow himself a full night's sleep. He was tired, but grateful to his mystery benefactors.

Halfway through that week, as his second batch of super crops began to reach maturity, he went out into the far barn to look for some of his dad's old tools. When he emerged, he looked towards the shining metal fence. What he saw made him drop the old toolbox in surprise. There, stood watching him, was a tall slim man in a long dark coat and wearing a wide brimmed hat. The figure was too far away for him to make out any of his features but he was just stood watching him.

Was this one of the people who was responsible for all of this? If so, David felt like running over there and kissing them. He decided, though, that a friendly wave was a much better way to go. He raised his arm and smiled at the figure. For a few moments, the figure remained motionless, just observing him, then slowly he raised his arm and returned the gesture. David nodded then lowered his arm; the figure turned and ran towards the copse. Part of David wanted to follow this stranger. He wanted to know who he was, and why they had chosen him. He thought better of this, though, he couldn't afford to be too curious, otherwise they might reclaim their gift.

David felt simultaneously elated that his money problems were disappearing and exhausted from the lack of sleep. However, he could not wait to take the cheques into the bank after the next harvest. He wanted to see the look of disappointment on that smug prick Porter's face as he realised the bank would not be taking the farm from him. He thought even though it was only Wednesday he might head out into town that evening, to celebrate his new found success, and drink a toast to his mysterious helpers.

He did just that, he drove his four by four into Sleaford at about seven thirty, he would leave it there overnight, and get a taxi home. He first went to the Barge and Bottle and ate his first proper meal in weeks. He loved their deep fried brie, which he had as a starter, followed by a mixed grill, and for dessert, he opted for the baked cheesecake. After the meal he sat and had a few drinks in the Barge, but decided to move on quite quickly. It was a reasonable place to eat, but he never enjoyed it much as a pub. Instead he crossed through Money's Yard and walked up Southgate and went to the Nag's Head. This place had gone down hill recently, complaints about noise from petty neighbours meant that they never opened the small club they had upstairs anymore. This had led people to drink elsewhere, but David still liked the place. He took a seat at the bar and ordered a pint of John Smith's. He had all night, there was no need to hit the whiskey just yet.

He had a pleasant enough night, there were a few familiar faces out and about and he enjoyed the company and conversation. There was more variety of people in town than in the village pub. In there, you were guaranteed to see the same few faces night after night. By the time the Nag's closed at midnight he was feeling quite well oiled. Not paralytic, but pretty tipsy. He supposed part of it was his good mood and the company. Of late, he had been drinking to ease stress and worry, not for enjoyment. He walked up Southgate to the taxi rank near the train station. He recognised Alan, the taxi driver who lived in the village, waiting at the rank and walked over.

'Hello, Mr Barker,' Alan said with a smile as David reached his window.

'Evening, Alan, how much to get me home?' David asked.

'Eighteen pounds unfortunately, Mr Barker,' Alan said. 'It's after midnight.'

'No problem, Al,' David said getting into the passenger seat. 'Money is not a problem tonight.'

The drive from the taxi rank to his farm took about fifteen minutes. David asked Alan about his family, how they were and so on. Alan told him, in depth, how each of them was. David sat and listened, he had forgotten just how many children the taxi driver had, but still it was more company and conversation, and after the months of isolation at the farm, it was even a pleasure to listen to Alan bang on about his kids.

When they reached the farm, David pulled out his wallet. He handed over a fifty pound note and told Alan to keep the change. At first, the taxi driver refused, saying it was too much of a tip, but eventually David persuaded him to take it. David stood out the front of the house, inhaling the pleasantly warm air. It was so still and quiet. He checked his watch and saw that it was nearly quarter to one. The commotion in the far field would begin in an hour and a quarter—two in the morning, every night, on the dot.

He found himself, in his inebriated state, getting curious as to who his mysterious friends were? Why they had picked him? And just what the hell were they doing in the far field? He had seen that figure by the fence that morning; they had waved at each other. The figure had been dressed oddly for a farmer, in a long dark coat and a wide brimmed hat. To David he had looked more like a spy than a farmer.

The Government. Was that the answer? Were they conducting some cloak and dagger experiments in the far field? Something to do with genetically modified crops, perhaps? There had been a huge backlash against that sort of thing in the media, so it would explain the secrecy. Or, maybe they were testing some kind of super fertliser, something that could make crops grow from seed to harvest in a week. That would explain his crops.

What were the potential dangers of this, though? David had already started selling his crops. If they were the result of some top secret Government experiment then there could be health risks. The public were so conscious about their food at the moment, what with the whole horse meat in beef burgers panic. What if the crops he sold drove you mad or gave you cancer? The Government would deny all knowledge and he would be left taking the flack, with no answers to give. The money he was making would be worth nothing when the lawsuits started. He would be ruined.

Suddenly he felt less genial towards his helpers, after all, they could easily be setting him up for the fall if everything went pear shaped. He needed to know what was happening in the far field, and he needed to know right then.

He took the ladder that was still propped up against the front of the house. He walked with it around the house, across the courtyard, and past the barns and outbuildings. He then headed towards the metal fence at the southern edge of the far field.

He propped the ladder up against the fence and started his ascent. To his pleasant surprise, the ladder reached all the way to the top of the fence. He tried to peer down into the field, but it was a new moon and the light was dim. He wished he had brought a torch out with him, but he did not have time to go and get one and come back. The fence itself was actually more like a wall. It was thick enough for him to sit on at the top and dangle his legs over the other side. Sober, he might have thought how dangerous this whole thing was, but in his current state he decided to pull the ladder up and set it down on the other side. He began to climb down.

He stopped with a jolt half way down. He had heard a sound, a sound that made no sense, not in a field at night. He was sure he had heard the faint cry of a newborn baby. He listened intently for a few moments, waiting to see if the sound came again. It did not. He figured that it must have been a sound from one of the houses down the lane, carried on the wind. Sounds had a funny way of traveling at night, especially in such a flat area.

He continued his descent and stepped off the ladder. The ground below him felt like normal earth. He looked around. In the dim light he could make out rows upon rows of dark shapes. They were plants of some kind, though he could not imagine what. They each stood at least ten feet tall, and their stalks were as thick as a young birch tree. They had large, fanning leaves. To David they most resembled palm leaves, though they were completely the wrong shape, far too rounded. Each plant also seemed to hold about five strange lumpy fruit, about the size of marrows. In the gloom, he could not make out much detail. He remembered that he had a lighter on him. He had officially given up smoking years ago, but still carried a lighter whenever he went on a night out, as he would indulge in the odd cigar. He began searching his pockets.

There was a scuttling sound off to his right, about fifty yards away at a guess. There was no way in this light he could possibly see what it was. He knew full well, though, that the area was full of rabbits and foxes, both of which would find a way into the field under the fence.

He continued his search for the lighter. When he found it, he walked closer to the nearest plant to him. He stood in front of it and struck the wheel on the Zippo. The flickering light of the flame illuminated the plant a little. David couldn't be sure, because flames have a way of distorting colours, but he was pretty sure that those palm like leaves were blue. In all his life, even in his time at university, he had never heard of a plant this size with blue leaves; come to think of it, he couldn't remember ever hearing of any plant with blue leaves.

The scuttling sounds came again, closer this time, and there were more, they were off to his right and left now. He felt a little unnerved; rabbits would usually run a mile at the merest hint of a human, not get closer. He now suspected they were definitely foxes, and if there were enough of them, they'd be able to give him some nasty bites.

'Piss off!' he yelled at the top of his voice. It worked; he heard them scurry away at the sound.

He re-struck the lighter and continued to examine the plant. This time he focused on those large lumpy fruits. They were dark green, and mottled with a deep red. They were fascinating. They had a rounded piece at the top that was attached to the plant by a thick stalk, like on a pumpkin. This flowed into a longer section, which did quite resemble a marrow. Four long, thin prongs protruded from the midsection. It was almost shaped like a person. He remembered stories from his childhood of mandrakes, the living, humanoid plants that screamed when they were pulled from the ground. He was sure that in the stories, though, they had been some kind of root vegetable, not a fruit that grew on trees. He was not sure if they were even real, or just some old wives tale.

The scuttling returned in force, there must have been at least half a dozen foxes out there in the darkness. They had edged closer to him this time.

'Shoo, you bastards!' he screamed at the top of his lungs, hearing his voice echo around the field as it bounced off the metal wall. Once more, they scurried away.

David struck the lighter again, the wheel was getting hot now, but at least due to the heavy, metal casing, the lighters body remained cool. He looked at the fruit again, moving even closer. He held the light against the top of the fruit where the pumpkin like stalk joined the plant. On this rounded section there were a series of raised bumps and slits, he looked carefully and saw how much they resembled a rudimentary face—eyes, yes, but closed; a nose, yes, but small and a mouth, narrow and shut.

He felt a chill run down his spine, he had no idea what these plants were, but they made him feel uncomfortable. Yet, with his lighter in hand, he could not stop looking at it.

With horror he saw that the fruit was looking at him, the closed eye slits had opened, revealing large, almond shaped, milky grey eyes. David opened his mouth to scream in shock, but before he could, the fruit opened its mouth slit. It was much wider when opened; it revealed rows of razor sharp, black teeth. The plant screamed. The sound was piercing and made David's ears hurt. He fell backwards in shock, the lighter dropping to the ground next to him. Miraculously it stayed lit. He heard the scuttling again, this time from all directions.

The last thing he saw was at least twenty of these sinister plant creatures crawling toward him on all fours, their eyes emitting a slight glow, and their mouths open wide, and salivating. Suddenly a whoosh of wind extinguished the flame, and David was plunged into darkness, and then the agony began. His screams echoed around the far field.

Zala opened the magno-seal on the door and it slid open, allowing entry to the field. In the air above, the ship lit up the ground. Zala saw the irrigation tubes lowering into place, filled with the water, minerals and nutrients that made this fallow land more like the rich soil of home. Zala took off the heavy coat and hat, and removed the human facemask. It was uncomfortable and Zala did not enjoy wearing it, but the need for secrecy was paramount.

Zala stepped into the field and saw straight away the remains of the farmer, what little the young ones had left. There were some blood stained rags that had once been the man's clothing, some of the larger bones and the head. They had devoured everything else. Zala wondered how many had ripened tonight. They were growing so quickly here. Something about this planet seemed to agree with the birthing trees.

Zala reported to the captain of the ship that more young ones had ripened, and that the farmer was dead. The captain said for Zala to remain on the edge of the field and not let any out. A capture crew would be sent down to recover them. Zala had never understood why his race, which was so peaceful and benevolent in maturity, started out as these vicious little monsters. It was one of the mysteries of the universe.

While waiting for the capture crew to arrive, Zala wondered why it had chosen to become a midwife in the first place.

A CAMPFIRE TALE

Darton woods were not overly large. If you got lost in them it would only take you ten minutes walk in any direction to find an edge. That said, though, when you were in the woods it was still quite easy to feel isolated from the world. The woods were quiet, in some ways far too quiet for a place that was surrounded on one side by a housing estate and on another by an industrial estate. Yet even in the daytime, there was a great sense of quiet and peace within the woods. At night, this sense of isolation increased dramatically. If you were out there on your own at night it sometimes felt as though you might as well be on the moon.

Near the centre of the woods there lay the fire pit. No one knew who had built this area, but it had been there as long as anyone could remember. There was a large dugout pit; you could build a sizable campfire in it. Around the pit, a ring of heavy rocks had been carefully placed to stop the fire from spreading out, and there were three tree trunks laid at the perfect distance away from the pit. You could sit on them and feel the warmth of the fire, but without that sense that your eyebrows were burning. Whoever it had been that had built the fire pit, they had thought it out carefully.

For generations teenagers had been coming to the fire pit to enjoy themselves, away from their parents, away from the world. Bizarrely for a place like this, the teenagers always treated it with respect. It was as though they knew how special the place was, and how lucky they were to have it.

Mike, Chelsea, Alex and Sarah had all been there before. They had parties down there with large groups of friends, but tonight was different. Tonight was special. It was Halloween, and it was just the four of them going into the woods. They planned to sit there all night telling ghost stories and trying to scare each other.

Mike and Alex had gone into the woods earlier in the day to build the fire up ready, it was a given rule that if there was already wood in the fire pit ready to burn, that the area was in someway booked for the night. If anyone else had got the idea to go into the woods for Halloween and go to the fire pit, they would see the wood that the two boys had placed in it and see that the spot was taken.

So they were all shocked as they walked through the woods towards the fire pit.

'What's that glow?' Sarah asked.

They all looked ahead and saw the flickering light near the centre of the woods.

'Someone's lit our fire,' Alex said, the annoyance in his voice evident to all.

'Cheeky fuckers,' Mike said.

'Oh well, let's do something else instead,' Chelsea said. They all knew that she was the biggest coward of the group, so it was no surprise that she suggested this. Mike, on the other hand, was fuming. He had not spent two hours in the woods that afternoon collecting up the best firewood, and building it up ready to light, only to have some other group of pricks come along and take it for their own. He was not going to stand for that, and he led the march towards the flickering fire.

He was psyching himself up for potential conflict as they walked towards the fire pit. When they reached it, though, thoughts of violence were soon replaced by confusion. There was no other group of teenagers partying at their fire, instead there was one, solitary old man sat on one of the tree trunks.

He was tall and thin, gaunt almost. His hair was long and wild, and completely grey. He had a mustache that ran into his overgrown sideburns. His eyes looked sunk and tired. He wore a frayed, long, old coat. At one time, the coat may have been red, but now it had faded to a point that determining its colour for sure was virtually impossible. His feet were bare and he sat smoking an overly large, old pipe.

'Good evening,' he said, smiling as they approached.

'Hello,' Mike said. The others mumbled greetings.

'I take it you built this fire?' the old man said.

'Well, yes, actually we did,' Mike said. 'We were planning to come here tonight, so built it up in the daytime.'

'Very wise,' the old man said. 'Very wise indeed.'

The four teenagers felt uncomfortable. The old man sat there smiling and smoking his pipe for a few moments.

'I'm sorry I lit it,' he said finally. 'I was just passing by and saw it, I needed to take the weight off my feet for a while, and it's not exactly warm out tonight. Please sit down, though, and enjoy your night, I shall be on my way soon enough.'

They looked at each other. Mike shrugged and Alex nodded, Sarah smiled and nodded. It was only Chelsea who looked as though she didn't want to, but the others weren't surprised by this. Mike took her off to the side as the other two sat down on one of the spare tree trunks.

'I don't like this Mike,' she said, looking over her shoulder at the old man. Mike looked over and saw that their friends already had the beers out and had even offered one to the old man, who graciously accepted it.

'Why?' Mike said. 'What's the problem?'

'What is he doing here?' she asked, concerned.

'Like he said, he's just having a rest.' Mike said. 'He's an old man, they get worn out easily.'

'Then what is he doing walking through the woods at night on Halloween? Doesn't that seem strange to anyone else?'

'He's probably drunk,' Mike said, trying to reassure her.

'That's supposed to make me feel better?' she replied. 'What if he's some kind of pervert?'

Mike laughed.

'Then I'm sure that me and Alex could take him,' Mike said, smirking. 'Come on, we've been planning this for ages. Don't let it spoil the night. He said he was going soon.'

'Ok,' she said in defeat.

They went and sat on the one remaining trunk. Alex passed them both a beer, and Mike lit up a cigarette.

'So what brings you youngsters in to the woods on Halloween?' the old man asked. Chelsea did not like the way the reflection of the fire flickered in his eyes as he looked at her.

'We thought we'd come out here and spend the night telling ghost stories,' Alex said.

The old man smiled.

'Did you guys hear about the one with the hook handed killer who escapes from the asylum?' Sarah asked excitedly.

The others groaned.

'Yes,' Mike said. 'Everyone on the planet has heard that one and it's bullshit. I want to hear some true stories. Didn't anyone find any?'

There was embarrassed silence from his friends.

'Oh great,' Mike said. 'So we've come out here and no one's got any good stories?'

'I know a good ghost story,' said the old man. 'A true one, about these here woods.'

They all looked at him.

'Didn't you say you were going soon?' Chelsea said.

Mike nudged her.

'What?' She complained.

'No need to be so rude,' he said.

The old man laughed a little.

'No, it's quite right, young man,' he said. 'I am intruding on your party. I shall be on my way.'

He leant over and began to pull on his boots. They looked like riding boots.

Mike, Alex and Sarah all glared at Chelsea. Eventually she cracked.

'Wait,' she said.

The old man stopped what he was doing and looked at her.

'Yes, dear?' He said.

'I'm sorry if that sounded rude. Please, we'd love to hear your story.'

The man bowed.

'Thank you for your hospitality,' he said. 'I think I have time to tell you this one. Tell me have any of you ever heard of the circus massacre of 1908?'

The teenagers looked to each other, to see if anyone had heard of it. Then they all shook their heads.

'That doesn't surprise me,' the old man said with a grin. 'It was a black day in Darton's history, and one they were desperate to forget. So they swept all memory of Canbini's Circus and the bloodbath that it led to under the mat.'

The campfire flickered, but a cool breeze swept by. Mike, Chelsea, Sarah and Alex all leant in slightly, already engrossed in the old man's story and entranced by his soothing voice.

'Rodrigo Canbini, the ringmaster and owner of the circus, had begun his life as plain old Rodger Canby in the cesspool that was Whitechapel, London in 1856. His parents were poor, and the whole family went into the workhouse. Rodger hated it, being forced to do such menial labour; so as soon as he got the chance, he escaped. He lived on the streets for a while, that was no small feat for a boy of seven in those days. The streets were a wretched and dangerous place. Rodger survived by stealing food from the markets and finding good places to hide.

Eventually he fell in with a crowd of other street urchins. They taught him how to pick pockets, and it seemed that Rodger had a natural talent for it. Not only that, but as he got older he grew tall and strong; he was not afraid to kill to get what he wanted.

He did some time in prison when he was just sixteen, for beating up a rich old man and stealing his money and jewellery. In those days, they didn't expect young boys to survive for long in the prisons. They all had to fight for food; there were no set meals back then. All of his gang thought that poor little Rodger Canby would either starve, be beaten, or buggered to death, but he wasn't; you see, Rodger was vicious. Despite his tender years, he made it clear that no one should try and mess with him; if they did they would rue the day.

He was released four years later, no longer a boy, but a strong, scarred and brutal man. He rounded up the members of his old gang and told them that he was now their leader. There was some disagreement from the previous leader, but when Rodger slit his throat, everyone else seemed to get on board with the idea.

For the next five years, the Canby gang terrorised Whitechapel. They robbed, they raped, they murdered. They ran all of the whores and the protection racket. They managed to get every other criminal off the streets. It was their own little kingdom.'

The old man stopped and took a sip of his beer.

'What has all this got to do with a circus and Darton?' Sarah asked.

'We're getting to that,' the old man said, grinning. 'I'm just letting you know the kind of man we're talking about.

'You see, a lot of the other gangsters in the East End of London took exception to being driven out of Whitechapel by what they considered to be a mere boy. They had been criminals longer than he'd been alive. They all got together and decided it was time to get rid of the whole Canby gang. They planned an attack on the house they all lived in. It was a massacre. A few members of the Canby gang got killed, but Rodger and most of the gang tore their attackers apart. They would all be hanged for sure; so that very night they all fled the country, heading for Europe. That was the last anyone ever heard of Rodger Canby. When he returned to these shores twenty years later he went by the name Rodrigo Canbini, owner and ringmaster of the greatest circus in the whole of Europe.

'That was in 1891, Canby, sorry Canbini, was now forty-five years old. He was still a tall and strong man and just as vicious. He ran the circus on fear. His acts were barely paid, treated horrendously and kept in line by the rest of his old gang, who now masqueraded as clowns of all thing. I assure you, though, there was nothing funny about them. Anyone who didn't do as they were told, or complained in any way, or God forbid tried to escape, was executed in front of the others as a warning. Even the circus strong man was terrified of Canbini and his clowns.

'They toured the country for the next eight years. Every night when the house was packed, the clowns would come out and do their act first. Canbini had planned it so well, his gang had learnt the art of being clowns, juggling, acrobatics, magic tricks, they did it all. Once their part of the show was over, though, they would sneak away from the circus and start robbing homes in the area. There wasn't that much entertainment in those days, so most people would have been at the circus. While they sat enjoying the show, Canbini's clowns were stealing anything they had of worth.

'Not only this, but during the show, Canbini sent his contortionists under the rows of seating to steal people's wallets and watches. It was a tidy profit maker for many years. Until the night they came to Darton.

'What Canbini didn't know was that a young detective from London had put two and two together and was hot on the trail of the man he knew was the wanted murderer Rodger Canby. He had been following the reports of robberies across the country connected to the Canbini Circus. In Darton, he finally caught up with them.

'As the clowns started their show, the police moved in, circling the big top. They didn't expect Canbini's men to be so well armed. A gunfight broke out; many of the innocent people watching the show were killed in the crossfire. When they saw their chance, the other acts who had lived under Canbini's tyranny for too long turned on the ringmaster and his clowns. They forced them back into the big top and then set the thing on fire.

'They say Canbini laughed as he burnt to death, his army of clowns at his side. They could have lived if they had just given themselves up to the police waiting outside. Canbini was too proud, though, he was not going back to prison for anyone, and the clowns all gladly gave their lives for their leader.

'That was Halloween 1908 in the field just at the edge of the woods here.'

The story had been more violent and sadistic than they had been expecting. All four of the teenagers wore a shell-shocked look. They could not believe that something so horrendous had happened in their sleepy little market town, even if it was over a hundred years ago.

The old man smiled once more.

'They say,' the old man continued, 'that the ghosts of Canbini and his clowns still haunt these woods, and that on Halloween night, they become flesh once more, hunting for victims, hunting for revenge on anyone who crosses their path.'

There was stunned silence. Mike finally broke it with a nervous laugh.

'That was a good ghost story,' he said.

The old man nodded.

'Well, I have taken up enough of your precious time,' he said, standing up. 'Enjoy the rest of your evening.' He bent down and picked up a top hat from behind the tree trunk he was sat on. He slipped it on top of his head, and for the first time they all saw just how tall this old man was. He winked at them and then headed off into the darkness of the trees.

'You believe that story?' Alex said.

'No,' Mike said laughing. 'It's bullshit. The old guy was just trying to scare us.'

Chelsea shook her head.

'Did you see his hat? And his boots? He was dressed like an old time ringmaster,' she said.

Mike laughed.

'Of course he was. That was why he told us the story, he knew it would freak us out,' he said. 'Or do you think we just saw a ghost?'

'He said they weren't ghosts on Halloween, he said they became flesh.'

'And I say bullshit,' Mike said. 'Throw me another beer.'

Alex threw him another beer and they began to talk once more, gradually relaxing and enjoying their evening, completely unaware of the army of clowns circling the campfire from the tree line, waiting for the right moment to strike.

AFTERWORD

I hope you all enjoyed this collection of stories from the Dark County and that reading them gave you as much pleasure as writing them gave me. I made the decision that my second book would be a collection of short stories, because after spending a year or so on my debut novel I wanted to write something more varied, to explore more elements of the horror genre and more dark corners of my own imagination.

The beauty, in my opinion, of writing short stories is that it allows you to investigate a single idea, without the need for masses of exposition or subplot. Whereas writing a novel is like a quest, writing short stories is like a day trip. It has allowed me to keep the motor running while I recharge my creative battery, ready for my next novel, which I will be starting work on almost as soon as I finish writing this afterword.

One thing I have always enjoyed is when an author offers some explanation of the inspiration behind their works. So that is what I intend to do here, let you inside my mind and tell you all of the things that got the cogs whirring as it were. So please if YOU HAVE NOT READ THE STORIES YET, DON'T READ THIS! Go back and read the stories. Okay, here we go.

A Drive in the Country

For many years, and to many people, I have said that Lincolnshire would be the ideal setting for an English version of *The Texas Chainsaw Massacre*. It has these massive flat lands and a sense of isolation. When you drive off the main roads into the really rural areas, you often see these dilapidated farms. For me it has never been hard to imagine crazed serial killers living in these places.

The kernel of this story actually came to me about twelve years ago. I wrote a script for a short film I never got around to making. In hindsight, it was a terrible and derivative piece, but the one element I always liked was the idea of a character who lures people to his home (and their imminent deaths) by jumping out in front of their cars. This was where the character of Smash came from. When I recently thought about this story I came up with something a lot more mature, and I hope frightening, than the original script.

Hoodies

Disaffected youth is a problem all over the country, but certain parts of Lincolnshire do seem to have a lot of 'chav' kids, who seem to enjoy intimidating other people. I have encountered some of the groups myself. Luckily, I have never been on the receiving end of violence from them, but the threat is always there, and they have made me feel uneasy in the past. This was what inspired the story. I didn't want to completely paint them as bad, though. The character of Benton is supposed to be our eye into this world. His reasons for wanting to be part of the gang, and behave as they do, are quite understandable. When society already has made a judgment on you, why try to go against it?

Also I really wanted to put the Devil into a story, he is such an important figure in horror that I wanted use him as a character, and I thought who better to dish out justice on these thugs.

The House by the Marsh

Of all the stories in this collection, this one is probably the most personal to me, hence why the narrator is called Chris (Chris and Kit are both derivatives of Christopher). Many of the things in the story are fiction, but a lot are true. The house did exist, pretty much as it was described in the story. I did find it with my friends when I was about fifteen. I did take photographs of it, that didn't come out, when I was doing my degree. The house was knocked down and replaced by a new house that within six months was boarded up for about three years. I have not been anywhere near it for a long time so i presume it is still there.

I wanted the story to hint at either the supernatural or mental illness being the cause of what happened in the story.

Fear and Loathing in Skeg Vegas

Anyone from Lincolnshire will have heard the term Skeg Vegas to describe our most famous seaside resort, Skegness. It is a wonderful place, with plenty to see and do, I look forward to taking my little boy on day trips there later in the year. And yet, in winter there is something very bleak about the place. I presume this to be true of all seaside towns. They are built for the summer, and in winter, they take on a ghostly quality. This is something I have explored in other stories before this, and I am sure I will explore it again in the future.

My love of Lovecraft and the Cthullu mythos is partly responsible for this story. I wanted to hint at a great, ancient race under the sea. I stopped short of describing the creatures, or even having them appear at all, as I did not want to find myself describing Cthullu; Lovecraft had already done this so well.

The incident in the story with the blue twinkling lights in the clear jelly like substance is true by the way. It happened to me one night when having a barbecue with friends on the beach. It was really weird, but strangely beautiful, and to this day I do not know what that stuff was.

Tracks

This story was the eighth story I wrote for this collection. I had realised that I did not have a ghost story (ironically, the last three all turned out to be ghost stories). Near where I live there is a railway bridge where the road goes over the tracks. One night, I was driving home on this road and my headlights illuminated a figure walking up the middle of the road about to go over the crest of the slope. As I reached that spot, I slowed down expecting this person to still be in the road, but as I went over the other side they were nowhere to be seen. I'm not saying I saw a ghost, but maybe; there were places to hide, but not many and the question as to why someone would want to hide is a subject for another horror story.

This event inspired me to write about a haunted railway bridge.

The Crows

Often when driving around the countryside you will see scarecrows in the field (surely I'm not the only one who has thought what if they are real people made to look like scarecrows? Or maybe I am). They always seem quite ineffectual to me, though, as the crows are busy munching the seeds, not giving the scarecrow a second thought. This was what gave me the idea for this story.

The character of Harper, the psychotic farmer, turned out very different than I had originally planned. I intended him to be a giant, uneducated brute, but he became an intelligent, well-spoken man, who took great care not to hurt the narrator too much and look after him in a weird way. I think this worked in the end, though, making the character and the story more disturbing.

Fear Thy Neighbour

On the road between where I live and our nearest town, there is a house. My wife and I noticed that they never have their curtains open during the day, but have them open at night. One of us, and I honestly can't remember which, suggested they were vampires. In fact, we still refer to it as the vampire house whenever we drive past it.

This was what gave me the idea for this story. I liked the idea of vampires hiding out in the countryside. It makes more sense to me than them living in cities. I also wanted to explore the idea of child vampires, in other works they have often been portrayed as being adults permanently trapped in small bodies. I wanted to explore the idea that something about the change from human to vampire not only preserved your physical age forever, but also your mental age. Hence, the character in this story, Timmy, is frozen in a permanent state of childhood and innocence, unable to develop or learn new things.

Coffin Hall

This story was inspired by two things, really. When I was about nine or ten, I had a couple of books of ghost stories for kids. I cannot remember the name of the books, or the editor or even the publisher. Of all of the stories, I only remembered one. It was about a young boy waiting for his friend to meet him. His friend was late and it was getting dark. He heard two old women saying what a tragedy it was about a young boy being run over and killed. Assuming it was his friend, the young boy races to his friend's house. Through the window, he sees his friend's mother crying and assumes he was right. Then his friend also walks into the room and he, too, is crying. The young boy races home and sees his parents through the window. They are in floods of tears. The young boy goes to try and find out what is wrong, but as he tries to open the door his hand passes through the handle. He was the ghost all along.

This is an old trick, but that story really stayed with me, I was reminded of it the first time I saw 'The Sixth Sense', and I wanted to try and write my own version.

The other inspiration is the hall itself. Coffin Hall does not exist, but it's based on Nocton Hall, near Lincoln. This was a family home, and then a military hospital, in fact my father was sent there while he was in the army. The house was set on fire and is now just a ruin.

What Grows in The Far Field

The idea for this story had been kicking around in my head for several years; I just could not decide on the right format to tell it in. Originally, I was going to write it as a screenplay, but realised that the story might seem stretched too thin over a feature length film. The idea reoccurred to me when I started writing this collection. As for the inspiration behind it, it was nothing more than my desire to write a science fiction/horror story. I am very pleased with the results, though, and think that this is my favourite story in this whole book.

A Campfire Tale

What is short horror fiction? It is merely an extension of the old tradition of telling scary stories round the campfire.

The inspiration for the story comes from the fact that every Halloween my good friend Chris throws amazing parties. His mother-in-law owns some woods, and there is a cabin in the woods where it usually takes place. It is generally an excuse for a lot of nearing middle age adults to behave like children and try and scare each other. There is somewhat a tradition every year that I tell a ghost story (My first novel 'Beneath' was actually based on a little story I came up with for Halloween about two years ago.)

About four years ago, however, we tried something different. We went to the communal woods in town and took some friends around there. Little did they know that Chris and I had arranged for some of our friends to be wandering the woods in clown makeup. I came up with a backstory to explain this, the Sleaford Circus Massacre. On the night, however, we decided it was more believable if we offered no explanation for the clowns. The story, however, remained in my mind. When I was deciding on a final story for this collection, I wanted it to be told around a campfire. The story of the Circus Massacre came back to mind, and I thought it fitted perfectly, because let's face it, clowns are fucking creepy!

I hope you enjoyed this section, and the stories in this collection. At some point in the future there may well be a Dark County: Volume Two. This place has more horrors in it. In fact, I think I have barely scratched the surface.
For now, though, I thank you for reading, and bid you farewell as I set off on my next quest. It's time to start the second novel, watch this space.

Kit Tinsley
March 2013

ABOUT THE AUTHOR

Kit Tinsley is an English horror author. He is a fan of all things horror.

He graduated from DMU Leicester in 2002 with a BA (hons) in Media Studies and English. Since then he has spent time teaching both subjects in secondary and further education.

He has also worked on several independent films, writing a film called *Red Route* in 2007. Unfortunately, the film, which Kit also acted in, has been lost in postproduction hell since completion.

Most recently he has worked on production of a film called *Shadows of a Stranger*, working with actors from the popular TV shows *Doctor Who*, *Rainbow* and *Torchwood*, as well as an actor who appeared in both *Batman Begins* and *The Dark Knight*. The film is being prepared for its release as we speak.

Kit is also a musician, He is lead vocalist/guitarist for a punk/folk/rock band called Dog Goblins.

He was born in Shropshire in 1978, but has lived in Lincolnshire since 1985.

He lives with his wife and their young son.

For more info, visit kit-tinsley.com.

coming soon

The terrifying new novel

THE

WILDS

BY

KIT TINSLEY